LOQUITA & RUCK

BY KAYDEN PHOENIX

Andrews McMeel
Publishing®

The authorised representative in the EEA is Simon and Schuster Netherlands BV, Herculesplein 96 3584 AA Utrecht, Netherlands. (info@simonandschuster.nl)

Andrews McMeel Publishing
a division of Andrews McMeel Universal
1130 Walnut Street, Kansas City, Missouri 64106
www.andrewsmcmeel.com

26 27 28 29 30 SDB 10 9 8 7 6 5 4 3 2 1

Paperback ISBN: 978-1-5248-9260-9
Hardcover ISBN: 978-1-5248-9261-6
Library of Congress Control Number: 2025946947

Editor: Hannah Kimber
Art Director: Jessica Rodriguez
Production Editor: Elizabeth A. Garcia
Production Manager: Jeff Preuss

Made by:
Made by: RR Donnelley (Guangdong) Printing Solutions Company Ltd.
Address and location of manufacturer:
No. 2, Minzhu Road, Daning, Humen Town,
Dongguan City, Guangdong Province, China 523930
1st Printing – 12/29/25

Written by **KAYDEN PHOENIX**

Art by **EVA CABRERA**

Coloring by **AKIMARO**

Lettering and Design by

SANDRA ROMERO

Written by **KAYDEN PHOENIX**

Pencil by **AMANDA JULINA GONZALEZ**

Ink by **ALEXIS LOPEZ**

Coloring by **VICTORIA ARAGON**

Lettering and design by

SANDRA ROMERO

CONTENT WARNING:

This book contains themes that deal with sensitive topics such as suicide, human trafficking, and animal abuse. If you or anyone you know is struggling with thoughts of self-harm, please call 988 from anywhere in the United States for help and support in English and Spanish.

LOQUITA

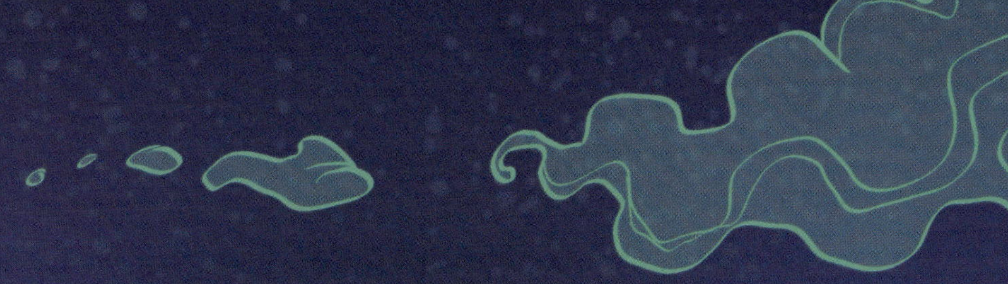

OQUI

Chapter 1

UM... HI...
...MINERVA. WOULD YOU, UM, LIKE TO GO TO THE DANCE WITH ME?
NO.
WHY NOT?
RIIINGGG
I DON'T OWE YOU AN EXPLANATION, GREG, I ALREADY GAVE YOU MY ANS–
PLEASE OPEN YOUR TEXT BOOKS TO PAGE 42, THE NERVOUS SYSTEM.
click
NOW, WHO CAN TELL ME HOW MANY NERVES–

BEEEEP
BEEEPP
BEEEPP
EVERYONE, GET DOWN NOW!
COULD YOU HELP ME BEAT VKYA?
PLEASE?
SHHH!
IT'S JUST A DRILL.
HOW DO YOU KNOW?
I HEARD THEM TALKING ABOUT IT.
IS IT ALL RIGHT IF YOU HELP ME NOW?
ZULLY, QUIET!!
WHAT? NO! JUST GO AWAY!
PLEASE, YOU'RE THE ONLY ONE THAT CAN HELP ME.
FINE!
BY THE WAY, YOU'RE BLEEDING.
HE'S COMING AFTER US BECAUSE HE HEARD YOU!
WHY YOU GOTTA TALK TO YOURSELF, HUH, ZULLY?

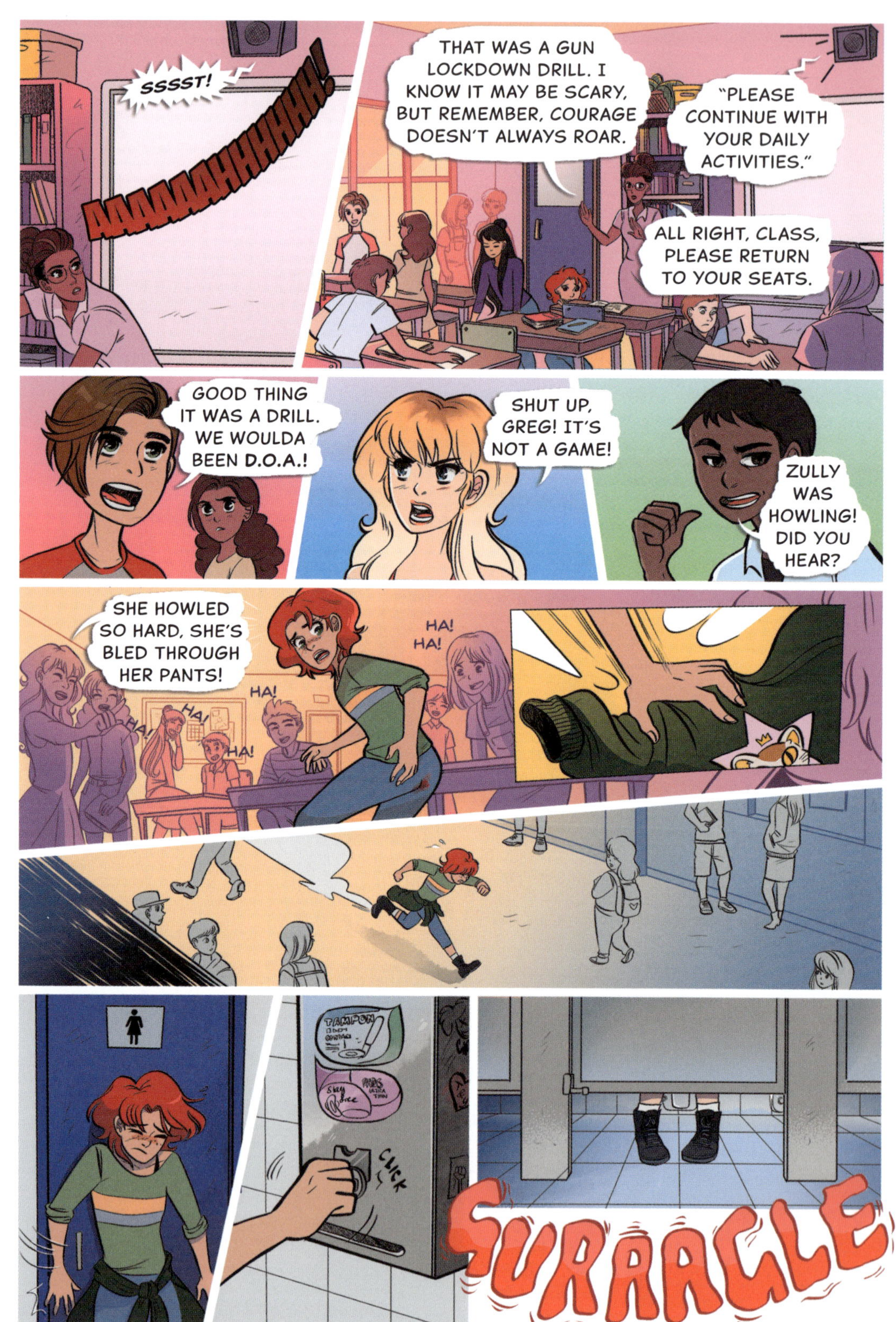
SSSST!
AAAAAAHHHHHH!
THAT WAS A GUN LOCKDOWN DRILL. I KNOW IT MAY BE SCARY, BUT REMEMBER, COURAGE DOESN'T ALWAYS ROAR.
"PLEASE CONTINUE WITH YOUR DAILY ACTIVITIES."
ALL RIGHT, CLASS, PLEASE RETURN TO YOUR SEATS.
GOOD THING IT WAS A DRILL. WE WOULDA BEEN D.O.A.!
SHUT UP, GREG! IT'S NOT A GAME!
ZULLY WAS HOWLING! DID YOU HEAR?
SHE HOWLED SO HARD, SHE'S BLED THROUGH HER PANTS!
HA! HA!
HA!
HA!
HA!
HA!
TAMPON
PADS
CLICK
SURRAGLE

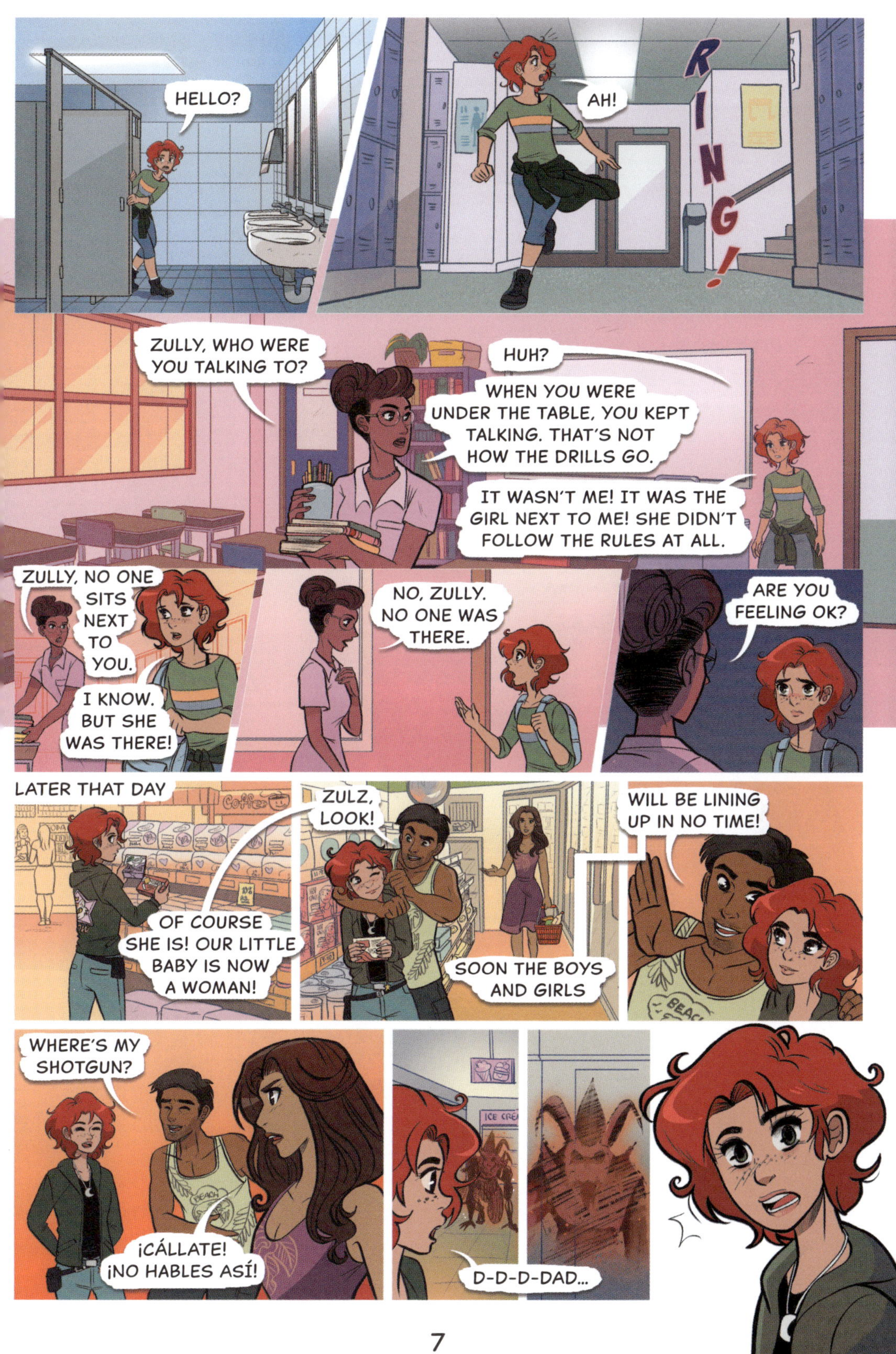
HELLO?
AH!
RING!
ZULLY, WHO WERE YOU TALKING TO?
HUH?
WHEN YOU WERE UNDER THE TABLE, YOU KEPT TALKING. THAT'S NOT HOW THE DRILLS GO.
IT WASN'T ME! IT WAS THE GIRL NEXT TO ME! SHE DIDN'T FOLLOW THE RULES AT ALL.
ZULLY, NO ONE SITS NEXT TO YOU.
I KNOW. BUT SHE WAS THERE!
NO, ZULLY. NO ONE WAS THERE.
ARE YOU FEELING OK?
LATER THAT DAY
ZULZ, LOOK!
OF COURSE SHE IS! OUR LITTLE BABY IS NOW A WOMAN!
SOON THE BOYS AND GIRLS
WILL BE LINING UP IN NO TIME!
WHERE'S MY SHOTGUN?
¡CÁLLATE! ¡NO HABLES ASÍ!
D-D-D-DAD...

THAT'S EXACTLY HOW FAST HE OR SHE IS GONNA RUN!

YA VEZ? I'M HIP TO THE COOL. I'M THE STELLA PARENT.
YOU DON'T EVEN KNOW WHAT YOU'RE SAYING.

ZULLY, HEAVY OR SUPER HEAVY?
MOM?!
WHAT?

SUPER HEAVY PADS FOR ZULLY!

GASP!

AAAAH!

THEY'RE GONNA KEEP COMING, YOU KNOW.
HOW DO YOU KNOW?

IT'S WHAT THEY DO.
WHY?
IF I TELL YOU, YOU MIGHT GET SCARED.

NO, I WON'T! PLEASE TELL ME!
WHO IS SHE TALKING TO?
THIS IS ALL YOUR FAULT!
NEVER MIND.
WAIT!
WHAT?! WHAT IS ALL THIS?
I CAN SHOW YOU.
WAIT! COME BACK!
I DIDN'T KNOW WOMANHOOD DID THIS TO A GIRL. WELL, I HAD SOME IDEAS DE LA LOQUERA, PERO...
WHERE ARE YOU TAKING ME?
DO NOT ENTER
THE SPIRIT SPACE.
STOP! YOU DON'T HAVE CLEARANCE TO ENTER!
HURRY!
WAIT, COME BACK!
DANG KID!
SECURITY
EMILIO

Chapter 2

SO WHEN DO I GET TO SEE THE... UM... SPIRIT SPACE?
YOU'RE IN IT.
HOW?? AM I...?
IT'S INVISIBLE, LIKE ME. YOU HAVEN'T EVEN ASKED MY NAME, YOU KNOW.
I'M SORRY, EVERYTHING HAS BEEN OVERWHELMING. WHAT'S YOUR NAME?
SISSEL.
SISSEL?
MY PARENTS LIKED IT.
THEY'RE NEW TO THE COUNTRY. WELL, WE ALL ARE.
COOL, WELCOME!
WHO DID YOU SAY WE HAVE TO STOP?
VYKA.
VYKA?
SHE HAS LITTLE ONES.
LITTLE ONES?
LIKE LITTLE DEMONS AND FUNNY-LOOKING GHOULS. THEY CALL TO HER AND...
...PEOPLE DISAPPEAR.

BUT HOW?
SOMETIMES SHE USES ENERGY, BUT MOSTLY VYKA ATTACKS YOUR THOUGHTS.
HUH?
LONELY, ISOLATED KIDS. THEY'RE SUS-SUSPECTABLE THE MOST.
SUSCEPTIBLE.
SUS-SUSPECTIBLE.
BACK AT HOME
WHAT'S GOING ON?
NOTHING.
UM...
WHAT HAPPENED TODAY AT SCHOOL?
OYE, CAN'T YOU LET THEM EAT THEIR FOOD?
WE'RE HAVING A DINNER CONVERSATION!
YOU CAN TELL US.
WELL, SOME GIRL IN MY CLASS—
GOT BEAT UP TODAY...

THE NEXT NIGHT

ALL SET, SWEETIE.
MOM, I DON'T WANT TO COME BACK HERE.
SWEETIE, AS MUCH AS WE WANT TO, WE CAN'T ALWAYS BE AROUND TO DEFEND YOU.
PARTICULARLY, NOW THAT YOU'RE A YOUNG LADY.
FIRST LESSON IN WOMANHOOD IS DEFENDING YOURSELF.
YOU GOT THIS, ZULLY!
I'M A YOUNG LADY NOW?
MOM!
YOU FORGOT YOUR TECHNIQUE ALREADY, HUH?
NO, NO, YOU JUST CAUGHT ME OFF GUARD.
WAIT, WHAT TECHNIQUE?

OH, WELL, MOM MADE ME GO BACK TO MMA TRAINING.
SO I CAN GUARD MYSELF.

RIGHT, PUES... FOR YOU!! TO KEEP YOU COMPANY.
I'VE NEVER HAD A CAT!

SHE WAS ALL ALONE DRINKING HER LECHE, SO I THOUGHT OF YOU.

AH, NO! YOUR MOM HATES CATS!

SLAM!
KEEP HER HERE FOR NOW. YOUR MOM DOESN'T KNOW I GOT HER!

I DON'T THINK THE CAT LIKES ME...
SHE'S JUST IN A NEW PLACE SHE DOESN'T UNDERSTAND. SHE'LL COME AROUND.

GOODNIGHT, ZULZ... AND LECHE.

CLICK

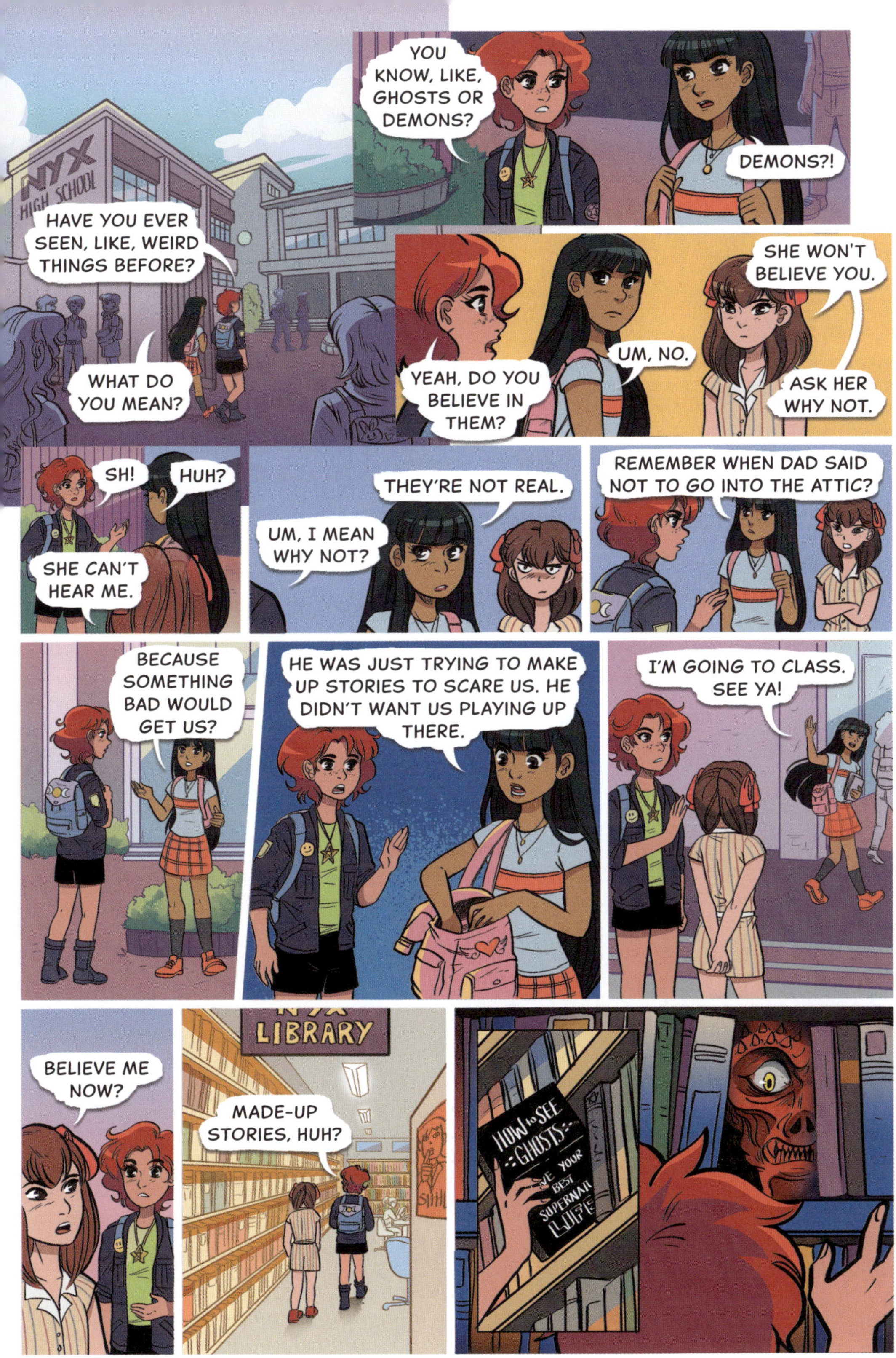

HAVE YOU EVER SEEN, LIKE, WEIRD THINGS BEFORE?
WHAT DO YOU MEAN?
YOU KNOW, LIKE, GHOSTS OR DEMONS?
DEMONS?!
YEAH, DO YOU BELIEVE IN THEM?
UM, NO.
SHE WON'T BELIEVE YOU.
ASK HER WHY NOT.

IT WON'T HAVE ANY INFORMATION YOU NEED.
THEN HOW CAN I FIGURE THIS OUT?
I DON'T HAVE MUCH TIME LEFT.
I'M JUST TRYING TO UNDERSTAND!
QUIET AREA
I NEED TO UNDERSTAND THE SUPERNATURAL. AND WHAT THIS FEAR CONTROLLING YOU IS. YOU HEARD TERESA.
"BEING ABOVE OR BEYOND SUPERNATURAL AND UNEXPLAINABLE."
YOU'RE RIGHT, THIS BOOK HAS NOTHING ABOUT THE SPIRIT SPACE.
I CAN SHOW YOU.
ACROSS TOWN
IT'S OK, THEY'RE JUST DOING THEIR JOB.
THEIR JOB?
THEY CONTROL BY FEAR. THE ONLY WAY TO WIN AGAINST THEM IS BY MAKING THEM AFRAID.

SO, LIKE, ONE OF THOSE?
NO, WATCH.
I'LL TAKE IT!

LET'S FOLLOW THEM!

SISSEL?

MY PARENTS BOUGHT FROM HERE TOO.

YOU'RE NEXT!

AAAHHH!

WHY DO ALL THE CRAZIES COME HERE?
MEOW TREATS

Chapter 3

LECHE?
LECHE?
LECHE?
I BROUGHT YOU YOUR FAVORITE. I'M YOUR FRIEND, YOU KNOW?
WELL, JUST KNOW YOU DON'T HAVE TO BE AFRAID OF ME.
ZULLY, IT'S ME. CAN I COME IN?
YEAH.
DAD SAID YOU HAVE A LITTLE CAT NOW. CAN I SEE HER?
NO.
COME ON! I WON'T TELL MOM!
SHE'S MY CAT, AND SHE DOESN'T WANT TO SEE ANYONE RIGHT NOW.
ZULLY, GET READY.
YOU'LL BE LATE FOR MMA.

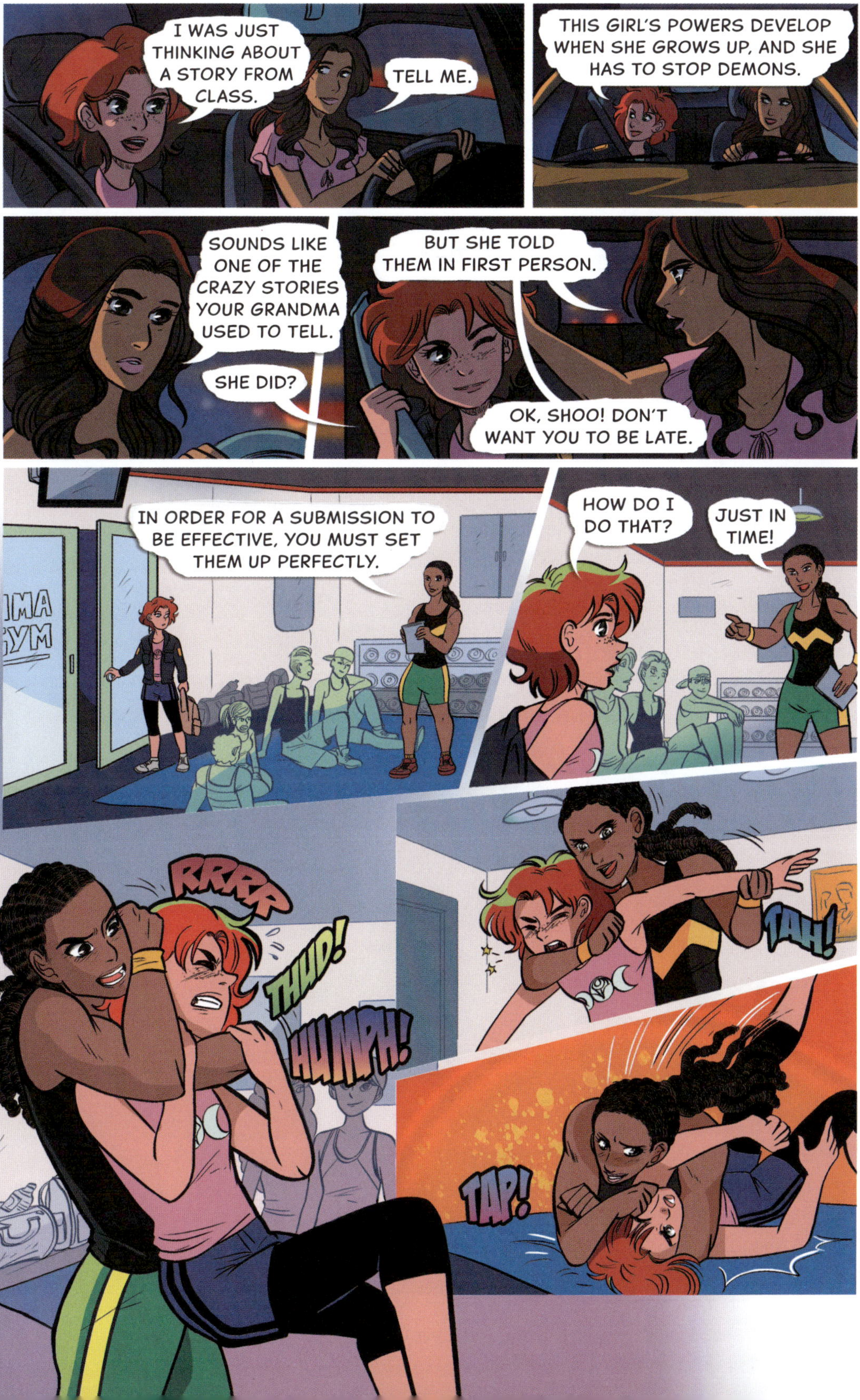

IN ORDER FOR A SUBMISSION TO BE EFFECTIVE, YOU MUST SET THEM UP PERFECTLY.

HOW DO I DO THAT?

JUST IN TIME!

RRRR

THUD!

HUMPH!

TAH!

TAP!

TIME OUT!
HEY NOW, THUMPER, YOU WANT TO LEARN SOME KICKS?
STOMP
I LIKE KICKING!
THE NEXT DAY
BYE, DAD! ZULZ, YOU'RE NOT COMING?
YEAH, JUST GOTTA ASK DAD A QUESTION.
OK, SEE YA!
WHAT'S UP, ZULZ?
PAPÁ, WHAT DO YOU DO WHEN YOU'RE AFRAID?
YOU FACE YOUR FEAR!
HUH?
WHEN I WAS IN COLLEGE, I WAS AFRAID TO BE ONSTAGE...

BUT YOUR MOM WAS AN ACTRESS, AND YOUR SCARED DAD WANTED TO SPEND TIME WITH HER.
SO, I WAS ONSTAGE NIGHT AFTER NIGHT CON TU MAMÁ RIGHT NEXT TO ME... BEST TIME OF MY LIFE.
I DIDN'T KNOW YOU ACTED.
OF COURSE. WHERE DO YOU THINK YOU GET YOUR ACTING CHOPS FROM?
MIRA, IF YOU EVER NEED CLOTHES, WE HAVE BOXES FULL OF STAGE OUTFITS, MASKS, AND EVERYTHING!
WHERE?
IN THE ATTIC. BUT DON'T TELL MOM.
WHAT IF I NEED TO LOOK SCARY? SO SCARY EVEN MONSTERS ARE AFRAID OF ME?
ADD SOME METAL SPIKES. EVERYONE KNOWS MONSTERS ARE AFRAID OF THAT.
METAL SPIKES?
SURE, WE HAVE PLENTY OF NAILS IN THE TOOLBOX.
YOU'RE A POWERFUL WOMAN, JUST LIKE YOUR MOM. YOU CAN TELL HER I SAID THAT.
THANKS, DAD.

BYE, DAD!
GO ON, ASK HER!
HE'S TOO CHICKEN.
HI, UM, TERESA.
HI. I GOTTA GET TO CLASS.
MY NAME'S GREG. REAL QUICK, I WAS WONDERING IF YOU'D, UM, GO TO, UM, HOMECOMING WITH ME?
OH, THAT'S NICE, GREG.
BUT, NO, THANK YOU.
HA! HA!
HA!
HA! HA!
DUDE, YOU CAN'T EVEN GET A FRESHMAN!
LIKE, WHO EVEN ASKS A FRESHMAN?
LAME!!!
HEE-HA!
HEYYY!
HEE-HAAA!

WHY ARE YOU SPEAKING HORSE, HUH?
'CAUSE SHE DOESN'T SPEAK ENGLISH!
STOP!
SHE SAID STOP!
I KNOW MMA!
AND I KNOW HOW TO USE IT!
ARE YOU OK? WHO WERE THEY?
YOU WANT TO GET ICE CREAM? I'LL PROTECT YOU.

IN THE COUNSELOR'S OFFICE

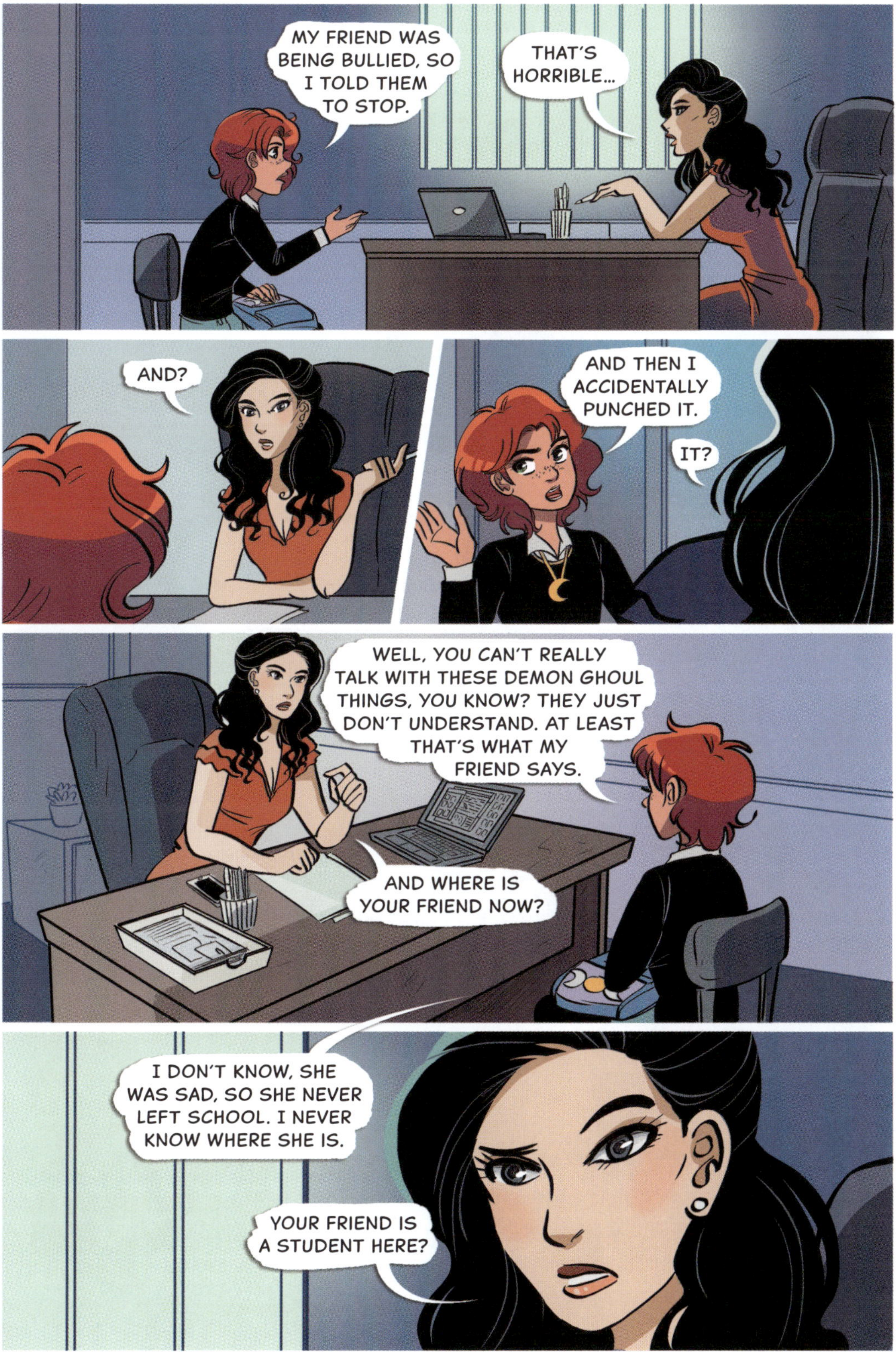

MY FRIEND WAS BEING BULLIED, SO I TOLD THEM TO STOP.

THAT'S HORRIBLE...

AND?

AND THEN I ACCIDENTALLY PUNCHED IT.

IT?

WELL, YOU CAN'T REALLY TALK WITH THESE DEMON GHOUL THINGS, YOU KNOW? THEY JUST DON'T UNDERSTAND. AT LEAST THAT'S WHAT MY FRIEND SAYS.

AND WHERE IS YOUR FRIEND NOW?

UM, I DON'T REALLY KNOW. SHE KINDA SHOWS UP WHENEVER SHE WANTS.
BUT THE SCHOOL GATES ARE LOCKED. HOW DOES SHE COME IN AND OUT?
NOW YOU SAID DEMON GHOUL THINGS...
SHRUGS

I SEE WHY SHE ALWAYS LOOKS DOWN NOW.
WHO? THE DEMON GHOUL THING?
NOOO, MY FRIEND. NO ONE UNDERSTANDS. AND I HAVE TO FIGHT EVERYTHING MYSELF WITH NO HELP.
WHAT ARE YOU SAYING, ZULLY?

?
I HAVE TO FIGHT THE **DEMONS!**

HELLO, PLEASE CONNECT ME TO ZULLY APROCHO'S PARENTS.

I KNOW YOU'RE ADJUSTING, BUT THAT'S NO EXCUSE TO TELL THESE STORIES!
YOU'RE HOME EARLY.
ZULLY HERE SEEMS TO LIKE SCARING EVERYONE AT SCHOOL.
MOM, THAT'S NOT TRUE!

THEN WHAT IS IT, HUH? DO WE NOT PAY ATTENTION TO YOU?
MOM, YOU'RE NOT LISTENING! I NEED TO FIGHT!
YOU WILL FIGHT AT MMA AND ONLY IN TIMES THAT YOU OR OTHERS NEED PROTECTING!

LISTEN TO YOUR MOTHER.

NO!

YOU'RE NOT EXCUSED!

IT'S JUST HER GROWING UP. SHE'S JUST FIGURING IT ALL OUT.

I'LL TALK TO HER.

SLAM!
KNOCK *KNOCK*

ZULZ? EVERYTHING ALL RIGHT IN THERE?
KNOCK
KNOCK

ZULZ. IT'S JUST YOUR LOVING OL' PAPÁ. YOU CAN TELL ME ANYTHING, YOU KNOW?

WHAT IF I COME FACE-TO-FACE WITH VYKA?
THEN, WHAT?

LECHE! I THOUGHT YOU WERE AFRAID OF ME!

I KNOW WHAT YOU NEED. A GOOD FUN MOVIE NIGHT!

¡ÁNDALE, VAMOS! BUT DON'T TELL YOUR MOM.

GRGGGGGGGRRRRRRRRRRR
POPCORN
POPCORN

EVERYTHING ALL RIGHT, ZULZ?
YEAH, UM, DID YOU— DID YOU HEAR THAT?
POPCORN
POPCORN
SHH! WE'RE TRYING TO WATCH A MOVIE!
THEN WATCH, CABRÓN! NO ONE'S STOPPING YOU.
YOU KNOW, THE SURROUND SOUND HERE IS REALLY GREAT.
GR
RGRL

GASP
AHH! NOOO!
COUGH *COUGH*
SOMEBODY HELP HIM!
BREATHE, COME ON! BREATHE!
AHH! NOOO! STOP!

BAM!
GRRRRR!
HUMPH!

COUGH
COUGH
COUGH
COUGH

SHE'S CRAZY!
WHERE ARE YOU?

SHE MIGHT BE A LITTLE LOQUITA, BUT SHE SAVED ME!

TO LOQUITA!

YAY!!
THANK YOU!!
CLAP
CLAP
CLAP
CLAP

EXIT

Chapter 4

GIRL POWER
GREAT JOB! I THINK YOU'VE GOT THE HOLDS DOWN.
HEEYAH!
TAP
TAP
FIVE-MINUTE BREAK, EVERYBODY!
READY?
ALWAYS!
STOMP!
ANYONE CAN DO A WALL FLIP!
WHATEVS.

WATCH!
HUMPH!
HI, UM, DO YOU THINK I CAN TRY?
YOU KNOW PARKOUR?
NO.
IT'S NOT FOR THE MEEK, KIDDO.
I'M NOT MEEK OR A KIDDO.
I'M A YOUNG LADY!
YOU THINK YOU CAN DO THAT WALL RUN?
DO LIKE I DID, BUT THIS WAY.
SHOW HER.
HAVE HER START WITH THE HORIZONTAL.
JUST FOLLOW ME!

HAVE A GOOD RUN-UP WITH FORWARD MOMENTUM.
PUT YOUR BODY AT A SLIGHT ANGLE.
ABSORB THE WALL. DON'T SLIP. GOOD GRIP. FRICTION.
GOT IT?
HUH?
LET'S GO.
STOMP
STOMP

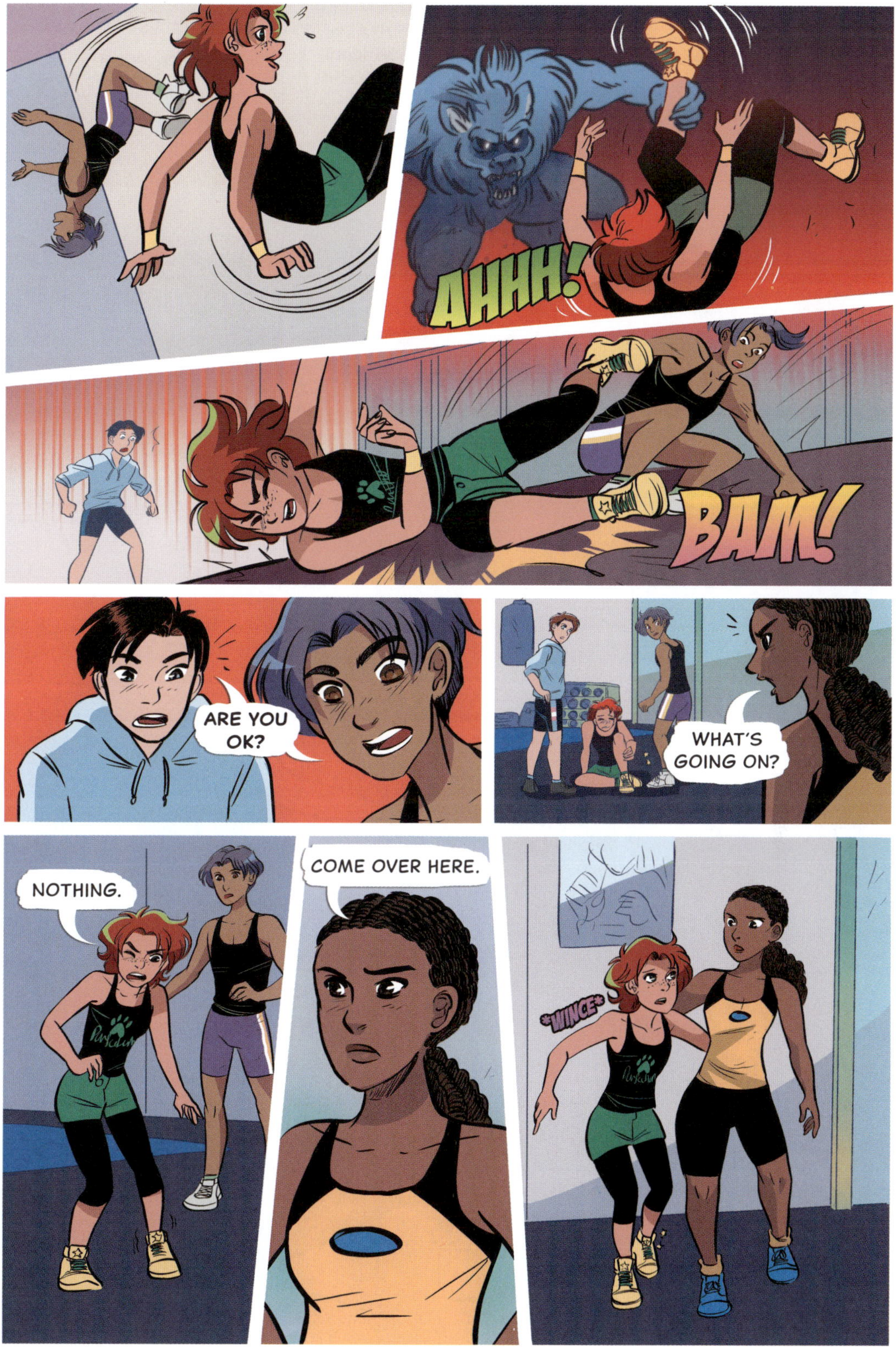

AHHH!

BAM!

WE'RE DOING KICKS NOW. I THINK YOU SHOULD REST.
BUT KICKS ARE MY FAVORITE!

PAIN IS INEVITABLE, BUT SUFFERING IS OPTIONAL. SIT THIS ONE OUT.
BUT—

LEARN BY WATCHING.

LECHE?
PLEASE?

LECHE

MOON
HI. CAN I SEE YOUR CAT NOW?
SHE DOESN'T REALLY WANT TO PLAY.
WHAT? SHE DOESN'T?

IT'S JUST, I JUST WANT TO BE INCLUDED. MOM AND DAD DON'T REALLY...

THEY DON'T PAY ATTENTION.
JALISCO

ALISCO
OH. WELL, UM, YOU CAN HELP ME LOOK FOR HER, IF YOU WANT.

YOU HURT YOUR FOOT?!
IT'S JUST MY ANKLE, DAD.
JALISCO

THAT'S EVEN WORSE! LET'S TAKE YOU TO THE HOSPITAL.
YOUR WORRIED PAPÁ IS GONNA FAINT!
AY, CÁLMATE. SHE'LL BE FINE. PUT THIS ON.

IT'S AN ICE PACK!
IT SHOULD BE HOT!

PADP!
PADP!

RRGRRGRR
HISSSSSSSSSSS!
POOF
zZZ
WHOOOSH!

Chapter 5

HEY, SLEEPY, YOU FEELING BETTER TODAY?
MA WAS PRETTY UPSET YOU DIDN'T GO TO SCHOOL TODAY.
REALLY?
WELL, I TOLD HER I HAVE TO TAKE THE DAY OFF TO TAKE CARE OF YOU. COME WATCH TV WITH YOUR PAPÁ.

GUNSHOTS HAVE BEEN REPORTED AT NYX HIGH SCHOOL.
LIVE
BREAKING News
VOL
65%

IT SEEMS A NINTH GRADER—
THAT'S TERESA'S GRADE!
THIS JUST IN:
A NINTH GRADER HAS KILLED HERSELF... IN CLASS.

GASP!

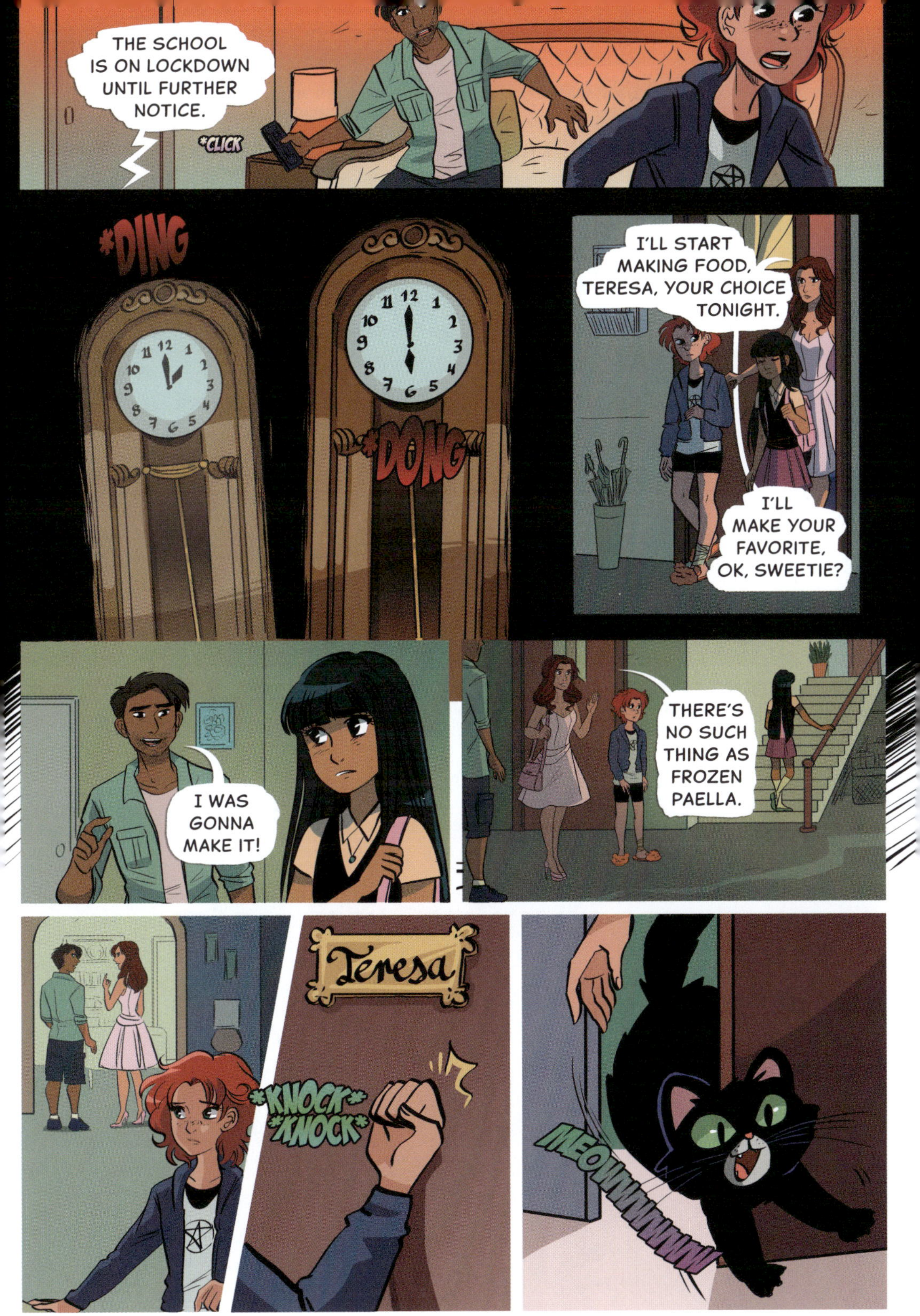

*DING
*DONG

I'LL START MAKING FOOD, TERESA, YOUR CHOICE TONIGHT.
I'LL MAKE YOUR FAVORITE, OK, SWEETIE?

I WAS GONNA MAKE IT!

THERE'S NO SUCH THING AS FROZEN PAELLA.

MEOW
YOU TAKE CARE OF YOUR SISTER, YOU HEAR ME, ZULLY?

YOU GO EVERYWHERE SHE GOES!
BYE, MOM!
DO YOU NEED TO GO TO YOUR LOCKER?

LOOK! THAT'S THE DEAD GIRL'S LOCKER!

HUH?

YOU DID THIS!

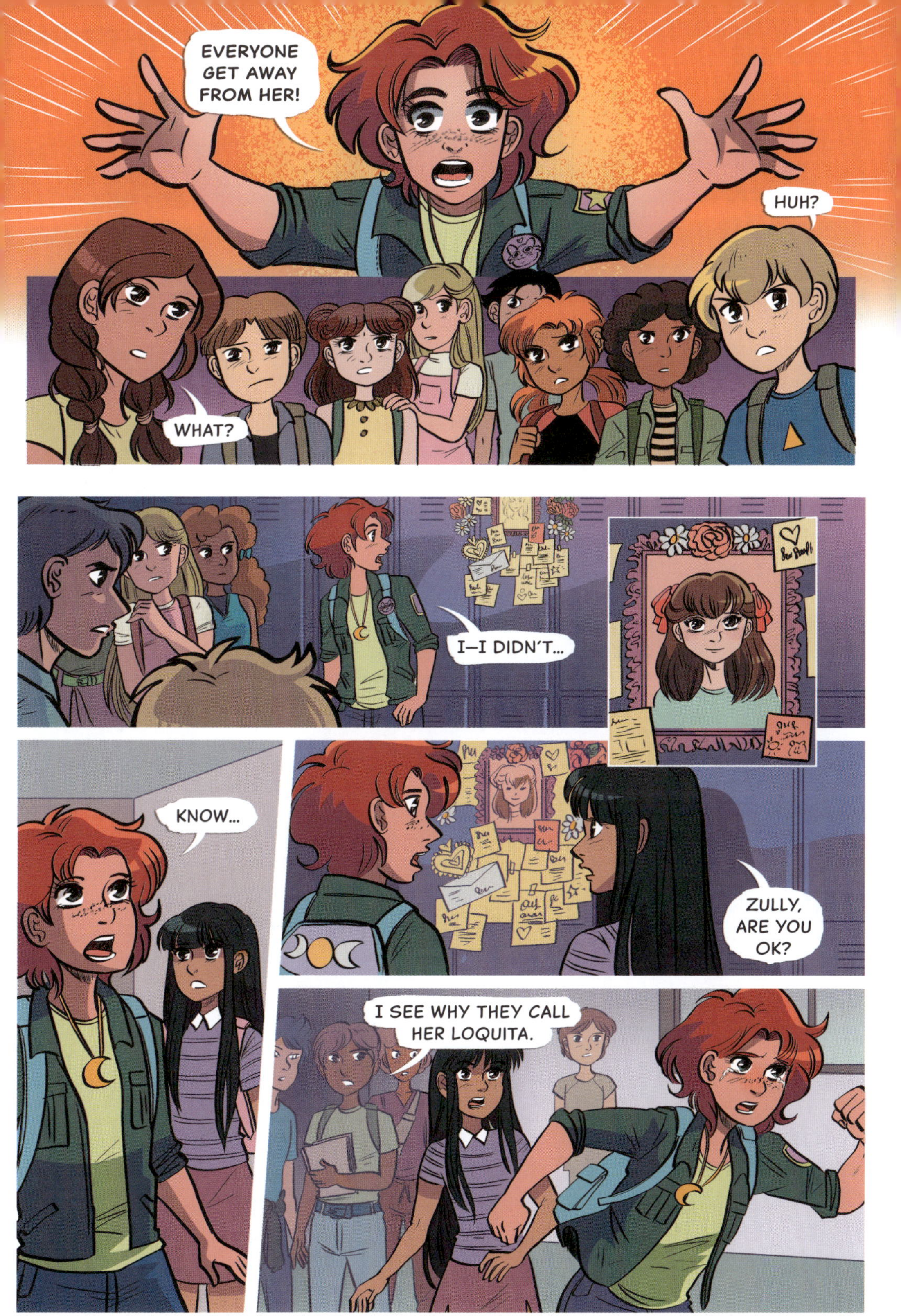

I–I DIDN'T...

KNOW...

ZULLY, ARE YOU OK?

I SEE WHY THEY CALL HER LOQUITA.

I DIDN'T SAVE THE LITTLE GIRL.

THEN SAVE THE NEXT LITTLE GIRL...
NO, NO, NO, NOT YOU NEXT!

THERE YOU ARE!

ARE YOU OK? ZULLY?
ARE YOU THINKING OF HURTING YOURSELF? YOU CAN TELL ME.

NO, BUT I WOULDN'T HAVE THOUGHT SISSEL WAS.
THAT DOESN'T HELP.

THEY MADE FUN OF HER ACCENT. THEN IT GOT WORSE.
YOU KNOW WHAT MOM ALWAYS SAYS, RIGHT?
WHAT?

COURAGE MEANS YOU DON'T LET FEAR STOP YOU.
SHE NEVER SAID THAT.

I KNOW, BUT IT SOUNDS LIKE SOMETHING SHE WOULD SAY!

EXIT
WE GOTTA HURRY.

GO AWAY!
YOU'RE A LOQUITA TO EVERYONE.
A LOONEY TUNE.
GOING RIGHT TO THE LOONEY BIN!
AAAHHHHHHHHH!

NO, I'M NOT!

SEE THAT?! TST! TST!
ZULLY! YOU'RE ACTING FUNNY AGAIN!

ZULLY!
WHAT?

CAN WE GO NOW?

BOO!
OK, BUT WE HAVE TO RUN!
GRRR!

SIGH

PRIVATE PROPERTY

HEY! YOU CAN'T–
SORRY!
I HAVE TO FIGURE OUT WHAT TO DO!

WHAT DO I HAVE TO DO?

PLEASE? JUST TELL ME WHAT I HAVE TO DO...

ARGGHH!
STOMP!

YOU KNOW...

YOU'VE ALWAYS BEEN MY HERO.

DID ALL OF YOU DIE BECAUSE OF VYKA?
WAIT, YOU'RE ALL IN MY CLASS.
EXCEPT YOU.
WHEN ARE WE ALL TOGETH—

PLEASE, TELL ME WHO IT IS.
I CAN'T SAY ANYTHING YOU DON'T ALREADY KNOW.

SO WHAT ARE YOU GONNA WEAR FOR HALLOWEEN?
I'VE BEEN THINKING ABOUT THAT.

THAT'S IT!
THE **HALLOWEEN ASSEMBLY!** RIGHT?
THAT'S THE DAY.
WE'LL SHOW THEM WHO'S SCARED!

Chapter 6

STEP
STEP
CREAK

TERESA WAS RIGHT!

AHHHHHHHHHHHHH!

IT'S JUST ME, IT'S OK!

ARE YOU LOOKING FOR MORE CLOTHES? WE CAN GO SHOPPING.
THESE ARE JUST OLD THEATER COSTUMES.
AHH, YOU KNOW ABOUT THESE CLOTHES?

OF COURSE! WHERE ELSE WOULD YOUR DAD HIDE THEM FROM ME, HUH?

YOU'RE GROWING UP RIGHT BEFORE MY EYES. JUST LIKE YOUR CAT.
YOU KNOW ABOUT LECHE?

WHO DO YOU THINK FEEDS HER? SHE CAN'T LIVE OFF MILK!

BUT DON'T TELL YOUR DAD.
I KNOW WHAT WILL GO WITH YOUR COSTUME.

THIS.

BANG!
BANG!
BANG!

NYX
HIGH SCHOOL
HAPPY HALLOWEEN

NOW, DON'T DERAIL FROM THE PLAN. STAY AT MY SIDE AT ALL TIMES!

SOUNDS GOOD, BYEEEEEEEE!
TERESA!
WHAT? I GOTTA GO TO CLASS!
OH YEAH.

I NEED YOU TO BE SAFE. FIND ME AT THE ASSEMBLY!
OF COURSE! I GOT YOUR BACK!
JUST LET HER GO.

RRRIIIIIINGGGGG
NOW **YOU'RE** LATE FOR CLASS.

MINERVA?
HERE!
GREG?
HAS ANYONE SEEN GREG?

BANG!
EVERYONE GET DOWN! THIS IS NOT A DRILL!

I'M HER HERO.

SLAM!
STAY HERE!
CLICK

BANG!
AHH!
AHH!

WHERE'S TERESA?!
BAM!

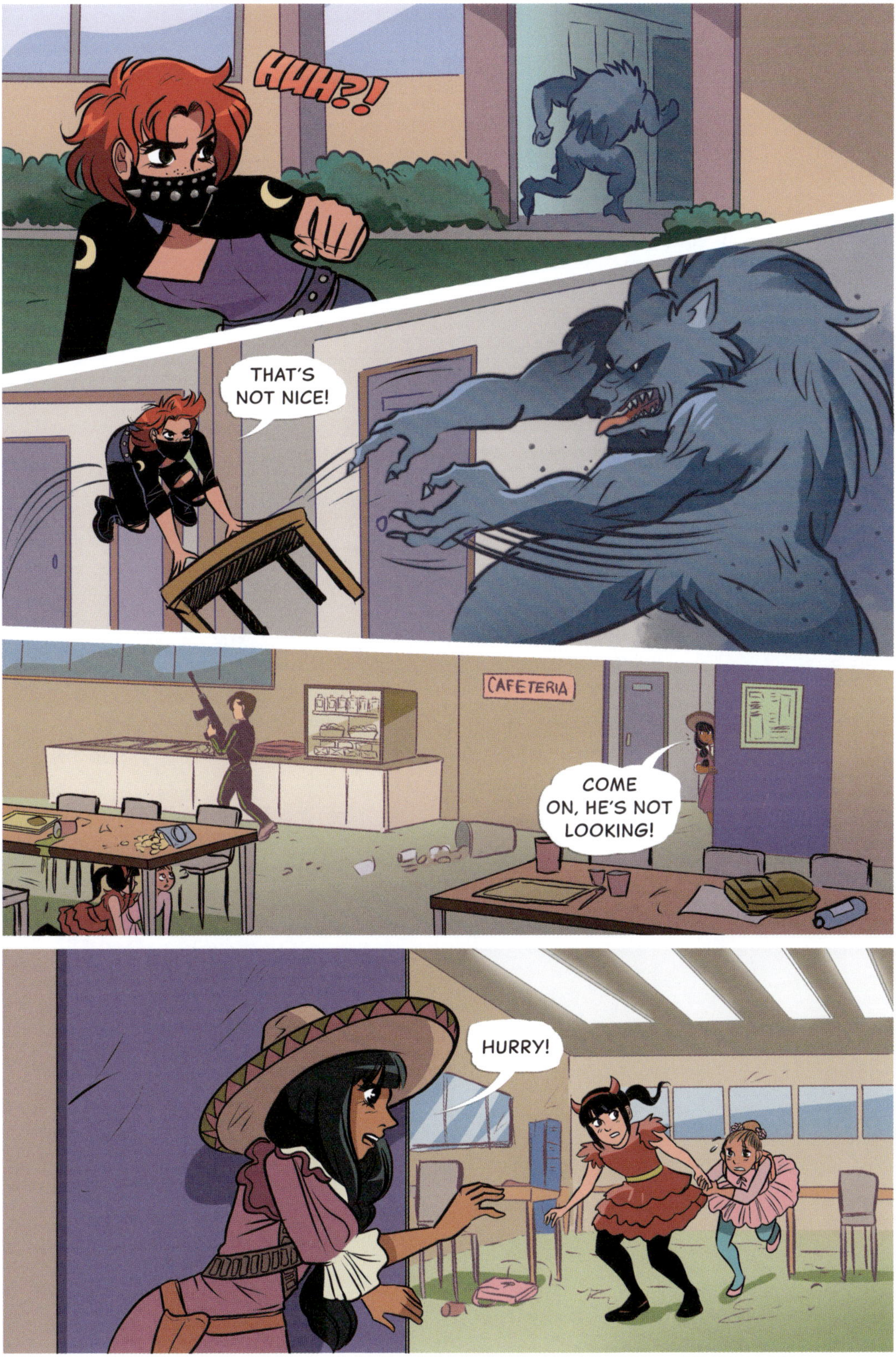

HUH?!

THAT'S NOT NICE!

GO THAT WAY. HIDE IN A CLASSROOM!

ERIA
PLOP

GO, GO, GO! DON'T LOOK BACK!

ERIA
CAFETERIA
NOOOOOOOOOOO!

I'M HER HERO. I'M HER HERO.

WHOOSH

WHOOSH

WHAM!

COME ON. THERE ARE BAD THINGS HERE.

WATCH OUT!

WHAM!

SO THEY'RE REAL?
YEAH. BUT DON'T TELL MOM OR DAD.
CAFE

ERIA
KICK

WHAT'S WRONG?

I WAS TOLD THERE'S SUPPOSED TO BE A BIG MONSTER.
BIG?
LIKE THE ONE IN CHARGE THAT TAKES THE SPIRITS AWAY.

ETERIA
WELL, YOU SAVED EVERYONE, SO THERE'S NO ONE TO TAKE.
UM, DOES THIS MAJOR ONE WEAR A BIG CLOAK, REALLY SCARY LOOKING?

YEAH, WHY?

I JUST SAW HER.
WHERE?
I CAN'T SEE ANYTHING ANYMORE. I THINK IT WORKS IF WE'RE TOUCHING.
WHO ARE YOU DRESSED UP AS?
I'M LOQUITA!
I CAN HELP!
NO, YOU DON'T KNOW HOW TO FIGHT.
WHOOSH!
WHOOOSH!
BAM!

YOUR FIGHTING IS USELESS!
POW!
BAM!
MOMMY...
YOU'RE GONNA CALL YOUR MOTHER TO DEFEND YOU, LITTLE GIRL?
I'M A YOUNG LADY, AND I CAN BREAK YOU!
BAM!
WHAM!
POW!
CRRRR

CRAAAACK!
POOF

SO, I FOUND OUT WHAT WAS IN THE ATTIC.
GHOSTS?
EVEN BETTER.

FREEZE!
THIS IS GREG. HE NEEDS HELP.

THE NEXT WEEK
HEY, SORRY I CALLED YOU LOQUITA.

I'M SORRY I CALLED YOU LOQUITA.

I'M SORRY I CALLED YOU LOQUITA.
IT'S OK, I KINDA AM.

SO IS YOUR MOM, AND HER MOM, AND HER MOM'S MOM. YOU KNOW, ESOS CUBANOS.
I HEARD THAT!

I WAS JUST PRACTICING LINES WITH, WHAT'S YOUR SUPERHERO NAME?

LOQUITA
LOQUITA

MEOWWWWW

AYE YAI YA! LOQUITA, YOU BROUGHT A CAT INTO THIS HOUSE?
BLACK CATS ARE MY FAVORITE. GREAT JOB, LOQUITA!
NOW LET THE PLAY BEGIN!

FIN.

CONCEPT ART

A
B
C
MASK
@evacabrera
Loquita
LA BRAVA UNIVERSE
LECHE the Cat

RUCKA

Chapter 1

Metro Local

HIGHLAND PARK
BUS STOP
YOUR
STEP

FRIDA CHIC

joos . bar
green
joy
joos
Open Mic Night
open

COFFEE

MENUS

HEY-YO! WHERE'S TEMO?

EXCUSE ME?

TEMO, HE WORKS HERE.
RUNS WITH THE 4TH STREET FLATS?

MISS?
UH... NO, SORRY. I GOTTA TAKE THIS ORDER.

UGH

fresh posh
fresh posh

Yoga Caliente

YANKEE Greens

STANDING bakery

WELCOME, FEEL FREE TO TAKE A "STAND" ANYWHERE!

EGHH

ROOSEVELT HIGH

GOOD OL' ROUGH RIDERS.

HOME OF THE
PRECIOUS PANDAS

I HAVEN'T SEEN A VETERANA IN AGES!
I AIN'T NO— UGH!

DID ROOSEVELT CHANGE THEIR MASCOT?

THAT'S PRECIOUS PANDA.
ROOSEVELT'S A CHARTER SCHOOL NOW.

TOP SCORING IN THE NATION.

TCH.

NO TEMO, NO DREA, NO ASH...

¡¿QUÉ?!

HEY VATO, QUÍTATE!

I'M TALKING TO YOU...

!

¡ÓRALE!

HEY

NO LOITERING.
MOVE ALONG.

I'M HANGING OUT.

NO. **LOITERING.** MOVE IT.
IT'S A PARK.

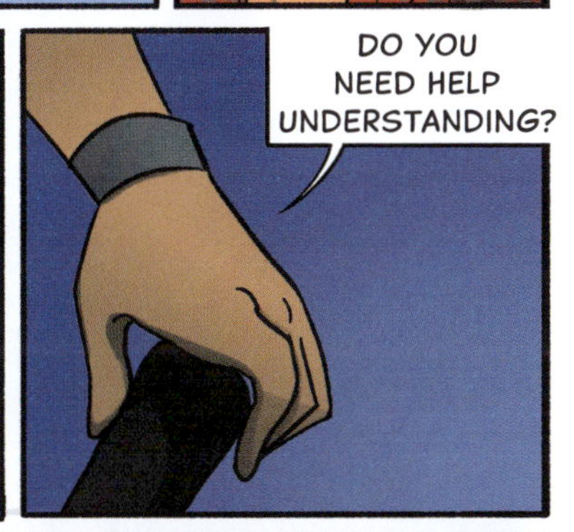
DO YOU NEED HELP UNDERSTANDING?

...

PIGS ARE STILL THE SAME.

MOM...
HOW COME YOU NEVER LET ME WIN?
COMADRE
RUCA
HOW'RE YOU GONNA BE GREAT IF I LET—
I DON'T KNOW!
EARN IT.
NOW, YOU WANT TO PLAY OUT FRONT?
CAN WE?
OF COURSE.
COMADRE & RUCA
HEY!
GET THAT FILTH OUTTA HERE!
THIS HOOD IS BAD ENOUGH WITHOUT GRAFFITI!

THIS AIN'T THE HOOD ANYMORE, LADY.

YOU BEEN AROUND HERE LATELY?
THOSE BABY SNATCHERS COULD STILL COME BACK.

MY NEIGHBOR'S KID GOT TAKEN THE OTHER DAY.
MISSING
BUT THEY'RE NOT TAKING MINE.

SHHH, OR SHE'LL FIND ME.

WHO?

ZIGGY!
GET BACK INSIDE!

GO CRUISE!
SLAM

WHITTIER
NO CRUISING

PRINTS $50
WE♡LOWRIDERS

Art Walk
THINGS REALLY HAVE CHANGED...
Henna by Haley
NATIVE DREAMS
HONK!
NOT EVERY-THING!

ELOTE

ELOTE N VIBES

MENU

STILL PRETTY GOOD.

MUNCH MUNCH

HNMPH

¿TE GUSTA EL ELOTE?
SÍ.

¿CÓMO TE LLAMAS?
ARI.
DON'T YOU KNOW NOT TO TALK TO STRANGERS?
MY MOM TOLD ME IT'S NOT SAFE ANYMORE.
WHY ISN'T IT SAFE?

'CAUSE—
ARI!
HI, MAMÁ!
¡NO HABLES CON MALA GENTE! ¡VENTE!

BYE.
HEY! I'M NOT MALA GENTE!

BUT WHO IS?

DONATE
WHERE WAS IT...

MISSING
THERE. THESE MISSING POSTERS ARE EVERYWHERE.

THEY'RE ALL KIDS...
¡HOLA!

WOULD YOU LIKE TO BE PART OF EL MOVIMIENTO?
??

WE'RE THE BUSY BEES!
WE'RE A LOCAL ORGANIZATION DEDICATED TO SERVING OUR COMMUNITY.
SIGN UP
BUSY BEES
PEACE • JUSTICE • COMMUNITY

WE'RE GOING TO FIND THE STOLEN CHILDREN.
WE'RE FUNDRAISING A TRIP TO SAN DIEGO.
FIGHT THE FIGHTERS NOT THEIR WARS

Chapter 2

VATO, WHAT DID I TELL YOU YESTERDAY?

...

YES, I'M TALKING TO YOU.

JEEZ.
YAWN

AW, DANG...

I'M GOING...
Z-ZIP!

¡DISCULPE, AYÚDAME!

MI HIJA ESTÁ DESAPARECIDA, CREO QUE SE LA LLEVARON—
Neda

ENGLISH.

HIGHLAND PARK
BUS STOP
GO ON.

SLIIIDE

YOU KNOW IF I ROLL A ONE OR A FIVE, IT'S OVER FOR YOU, RIGHT?

NO FAIR!
HAHA!
THEY'RE DICE, MIJA.
BAM!

YOU CAN'T CONTROL EVERY OUTCOME!
SOMETIMES IT COMES DOWN TO LUCK.
LOOKS LIKE MY BUS IS HERE, CHICA.

...WHAT IF THE DICE DON'T COME UP RIGHT FOR YOU?

DOING THE RIGHT THING ISN'T A GAME.

BE GOOD.

I'LL BE BACK BEFORE YOU KNOW IT.

San Diego

EXCUSE ME, YOU CAN'T BRING YOUR DOG ON BOARD UNLESS THEY FIT IN A BAG.

I DON'T HAVE A—

ARGH!

FINE.

WHERE'S A BAG?

BARRIO LOGAN EXIT

GET OUT OF THE BAG. YOU THINK I'M CARRYING YOU?

LET'S SEE WHAT WE CAN FIND OUT ABOUT THESE MISSING KIDS, VATO.

IT'S THE RIGHT THING TO DO.

HEY, CHICA, WANT TO TAKE A RIDE?

IN THIS JUNK?

HEY! DON'T BE TOUCHING MY CAR LIKE THAT!

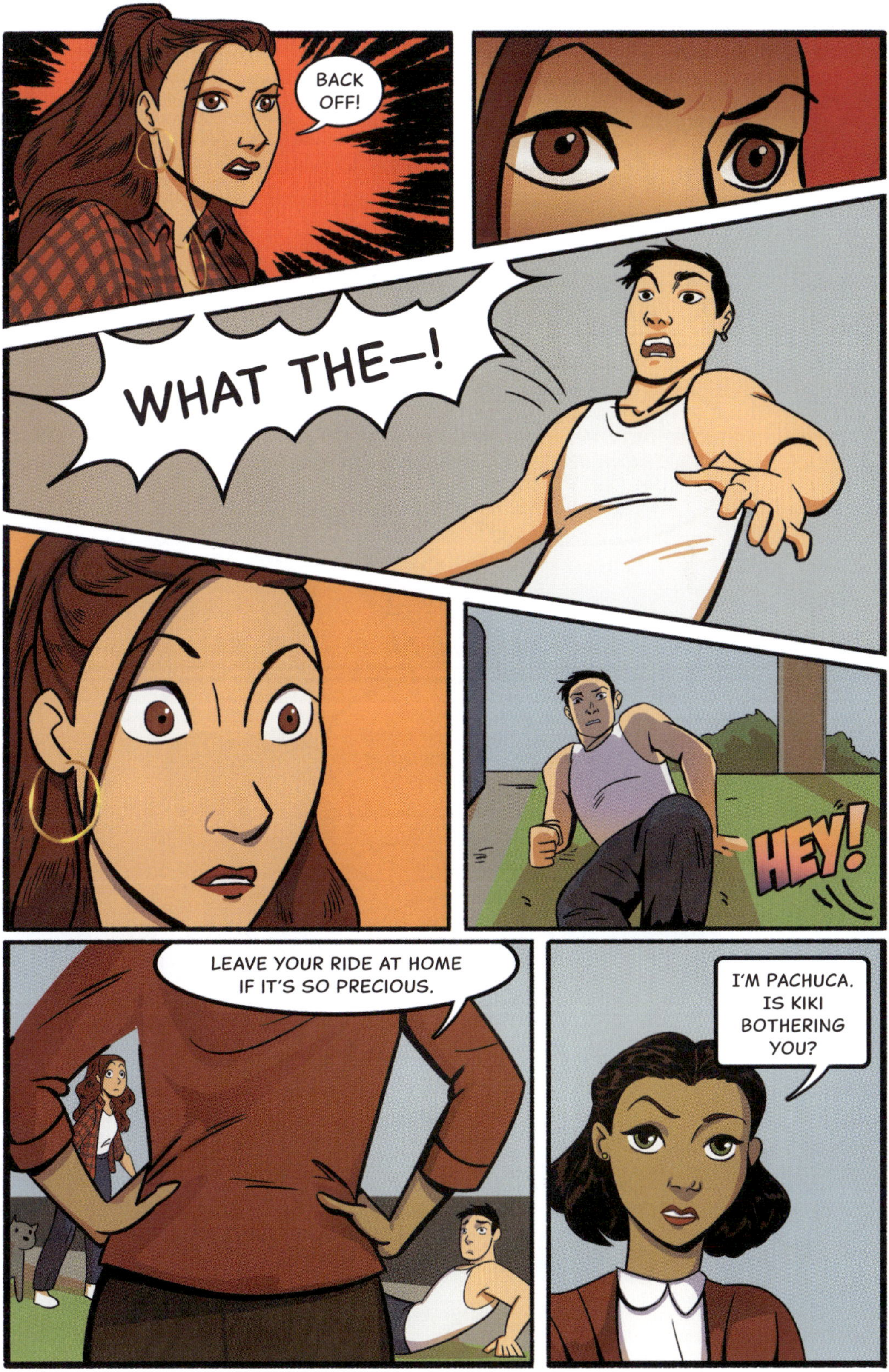

BACK OFF!

WHAT THE—!

HEY!

I'M SURE HE WON'T HASSLE YOU AGAIN. HE'S STILL EMBARRASSED I BROKE UP WITH HIM.

ANYWAY, WHAT'S YOUR STORY? YOU'RE PRETTY FAR FROM EAST L.A.

I HEARD THERE ARE KIDS THAT KEEP DISAPPEARING, LIKE, BEING KIDNAPPED. THE BBS THINK THEY'RE ENDING UP DOWN HERE.

YEAH.
SO IT'S TRUE! WHY HASN'T ANYONE DONE ANYTHING?
SHH!
WHAT?
LISTEN... WE PROBABLY SHOULDN'T TALK HERE.

¿QUÉ SABES?

WE SHOULDN'T TALK HERE.
HEY, LADIES, ANYTHING ELSE I CAN GET YOU?
JUST THE CHECK, THANKS.

HERE YOU GO.
YOU LOOK HUNGRY.

NANA, I TOLD YOU, WE *JUST* ATE.
WE SHOULDA COME HERE FIRST! GRACIAS!
OF COURSE! ANY FRIEND OF PACHUCA'S IS ALWAYS WELCOME TO OUR TABLE.

SO... THE STOLEN KIDS. WHAT'S THAT ABOUT?
YEAH, SORRY ABOUT EARLIER. PEOPLE... THEY TALK AROUND HERE.

IT'S ALL RUN BY A NUN.
A NUN?
YEAH, THEY CALL HER LA MONJA.
YOU GIRLS WANT DESSERT?
FRESH PAN DULCE!

NO, NANA! SORRY, SHE ALWAYS DOES THIS.

YOU GOTTA PUT MEAT ON YOU! YOUR FRIEND IS HUNGRY, ¿VES?

GRACIAS, IT'S DELICIOUS.
DON'T ENCOURAGE HER!

AT LEAST SOMEONE APPRECIATES MY COOKING!

HAHA!
YOUR NANA IS PRICELESS!
I KNOW.

ANYWAY, LA MONJA. SHE RUNS AN ORPHANAGE HERE. THAT'S HOW SHE KEEPS A CLEAN COVER, BUT US LOCALS KNOW BETTER. KIDS GO MISSING 'CAUSE SHE SELLS THEM.

WE HAVE TO GO THERE!
WHAT?! WE CAN'T JUST—! WHY DO YOU CARE SO MUCH?
DON'T YOU?

I... OF COURSE I DO. BUT NOBODY CAN ARREST THEM. WHAT COULD I DO?

MORE THAN THE PIGS CAN.

...
YOU CAN STAY HERE IF YOU NEED. BEATS THE PARK.

VATO TOO.

I HAVE CLASS EARLY AND THEN WORK, BUT NANA WORKS FROM HOME. SHE WON'T MIND.
OH, UH, YOU SURE?
MIJA!

I DROPPED MY PILL AND IT ROLLED UNDER THE STOVE.
WHEN I WENT TO PICK IT UP, I FOUND TÍA LICHA'S RING. LOOK!
MISSING FOR TWENTY YEARS!

IT'S PRICELESS.

HUFF
HUFF
RUCA.
WHAT–?
REMEMBER WHEN YOU WERE LEARNING SPANISH?
AND YOU THOUGHT RUCA MEANT ROCK?
CLENCH
AND NONE OF YOU TOLD ME FOR YEARS. THAT WAS MESSED UP.
I WASN'T THE BEST TO YOU.
I KNOW THAT.
BUT YOU'RE STRONG.

Give her her justice.

Give her her justice.

Give her her justice.

NO, DON'T!
MOM...

HERE. TO KEEP YOU COMPANY.
YOU CAN STAY AS LONG AS YOU NEED.
THANK YOU.

EVERYTHING SEEMS QUIET...

JUSTICE!

ANYTHING, VATO?

GIVE HER HER JUSTICE... I HAVE NO IDEA WHAT—
AHH!

THAT SOUNDED LIKE A KID SCREAMING!

!!
AHH! HAHA!

FALSE ALARM...
HEY, IS THAT YOUR DOG?

WHY, YOU WANT HIM?

MY MOM DOESN'T LIKE DOGS.
SHE HERE?
OVER THERE!
GOOD, DON'T WANDER OFF.

HAVE YOU SEEN ANYTHING, LIKE, WEIRD AROUND HERE?
HUH? HAHA, AWW!

TAG!
HEY! NO FAIR!
SIGH...
WE GOTTA FIGURE THIS OUT, VATO.

Chapter 3

EBT
MISSING
SMOG
HEY!
POW!
MOVE IT!
UGH!
JERK...
@#!%
OWWW...

YOU BEEN OUT ROUGHHOUSING AGAIN?
MOM...
WHAT HAPPENED TO YOU?

YOU DON'T GET IT, IT *HAD* TO... I–

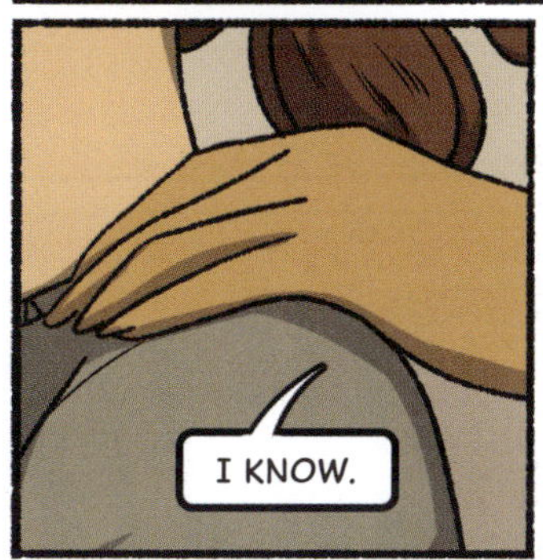
I KNOW.

YOU WERE DUCKING AND WEAVING WHEN YOU SHOULDA BEEN WEAVING AND DUCKING, RIGHT?
TELL ME WHAT HAPPENED.

THIS IS A GOOD ONE.
THIS PAYASO DIDN'T PAY THAT WOMAN FOR THE CAR SHE SOLD, BOUGHT A NEW ONE INSTEAD.
SO SHE SET IT ON FIRE! SAID "HE BURNED ME, I BURNED HIM BACK."

THAT'S **KARMA** FOR YOU!
LIKE... AN EQUIVALENT ACTION WHEN SOMEONE DOES SOMETHING.
PEOPLE GET WHAT THEY DESERVE.

LIKE JUSTICE.

HI, RUCA. HI, NANA! CAN'T TALK; I'M LATE.
GET DINNER FIRST.

CAN'T EAT BEFORE DANCE!
UH-HUH. SHE'LL BE HUNGRY.

YOU DANCE?

YOU WANNA COME?
HEY 'CHUCA!

SO WHAT'S UP WITH THE NAME?
HAHA! IT'S BEEN MY NICKNAME FOR SO LONG. I DON'T EVEN THINK ABOUT IT ANYMORE
I'VE ALWAYS LOVED THE PACHUCA STYLE! EVEN ALMOST WENT TO SCHOOL FOR FASHION 'TIL I CHOSE PREMED.

PEOPLE STARTED CALLING ME PACHUCA GIRL, THEN JUST PACHUCA, AND IT STUCK.

THAT'S A C-WALK! I LEARNED THAT LAST WEEK.

I WOULDN'T HAVE TAKEN YOU FOR A BREAKER.
OH?
I LIKE IT HERE.

THEY DON'T LOOK AT ME LIKE I'M DIFFERENT.
YOU KNOW THE WAY THOSE GUYS LOOKED AT US IN THE DINER, LIKE WE WERE... Y'KNOW...
KIKI LOOKS AT ME THAT WAY TOO.

MACHOS. THEY'RE A DYING BREED.

HAHA! I CAN BE MYSELF HERE.

YOU SHOULD BE YOURSELF OUT THERE TOO.

ALL RIGHT, CLASS! LET'S GET STARTED!

HERE GOES NOTHING!
FINISH STRETCHING! TODAY, WE'RE HITTING IT HARD! FIRST, LET'S DO...
HERE GOES NOTHIN'!

NICE!
L.A.P.D.!
STOP!
COME ON!
HEY!
CRAP!
GOT YOU!
RUCA!

I'M SORRY, RUCA...
THIS ISN'T YOUR FAULT, YOU—
WHAT'D I SAY ABOUT HANGING OUT WITH THAT GIRL, HUH?
THANKS FOR THE CALL, OFFICER.
NO PROBLEM, THOUGHT SHE LOOKED LIKE YOURS.
MOM!
AUTO SHOP REPORTED THEFT, FOUND THESE TWO RUNNING—
IT WASN'T US, WE TOLD YOU!
I HAVE NOTHING TO SAY TO YOU.
GO AHEAD, OFFICER.
NO, MOM!

JUSTICE
-karma
-lawsuit
-that folklorica chick

!
JUST A JOGGER...

OPEN
MENU
GET IT TOGETHER.

UGH.
WHAT AM I EVEN DOING?

I GIVE U—
THWACK!

DANG, LADY.

YOU A FIGHTER OR SOMETHING?

SORRY ABOUT THAT!
IT'S COOL! PROBABLY DESERVED IT.

SERIOUSLY, THOUGH, WHERE'D YOU TRAIN?
I'M CHICLE, BY THE WAY!

RUCA. AND, UHH...

HERE AND THERE.
HUH. NEVER HEARD OF IT! IF YOU'RE LOOKING FOR SOME PRACTICE, YOU SHOULD TOTALLY COME TO MY GYM! I'M KINDA THE TOP TRAINER.

OH, NO, THAT'S O—
SERIOUSLY! IT'S THE GYM THAT'S ACROSS FROM THE ORPHANAGE. WE JUST GOT NEW PUNCHING BAGS.

DID YOU SAY ORPHANAGE?

Chapter 4

THIS IS THE ONLY ONE THAT'S SURVIVED.
HAS GOOD FUNDING, I GUESS.

HEARD A NUN RUNS IT, THAT RIGHT?
YOU WANNA ADOPT OR SOMETHING?
AH, YOU'VE HEARD THE LEGEND!

SHE HAS THE POWER TO MAKE ANYONE DO ANYTHING SHE WANTS!
OOOOOOH

...
REALLY?

SPEAKING OF THE NUN...
I BET THAT'S HER.

RIGHT THIS WAY. SHE JUST GOT IN.
CREAK
IS SOMETHING THE MATTER, MR. GIBSON?
I HOPE YOU DON'T FEEL THE COMPENSATION IS INADEQUATE.
N-NO! I, UH, I APPRECIATE THE SALARY.
WE ARE VERY GENEROUS.

IT'S JUST, I THOUGHT...
I'D BE HELPING THE KIDS ALREADY IN THE ORPHANAGE.
NOT GOING OUT TO—
SHHHHH
THANK YOU FOR THE OPPORTUNITY TO BE A PART OF THIS ORGANIZATION.
WONDERFUL!
FRIAR BARBOSA WILL GIVE YOU YOUR FIRST ASSIGNMENT.

HERE IT IS!

THE GUYS ALWAYS LET ME HAVE THIS CORNER. NICE, RIGHT?

REMEMBER, AVOID A FIGHT IF YOU CAN. BUT, IF YOU'RE FORCED, YOU FIGHT TO WIN.

READY TO FIGHT?

THIS MAY HURT!

WHOOSH!

YOU GOTTA STEP TO THE SIDE AND DIRECT THE WRIST TO THE FLOOR!
WHAM
THAT WAS FIRME!
THAT'S NOT... I JUST DON'T GET IT!
YOU JUST SURPRISED ME. WHY YOU STILL GOT THOSE EARRINGS ON ANYWAY?
THEY'RE NO GOOD FOR FIGHTING!

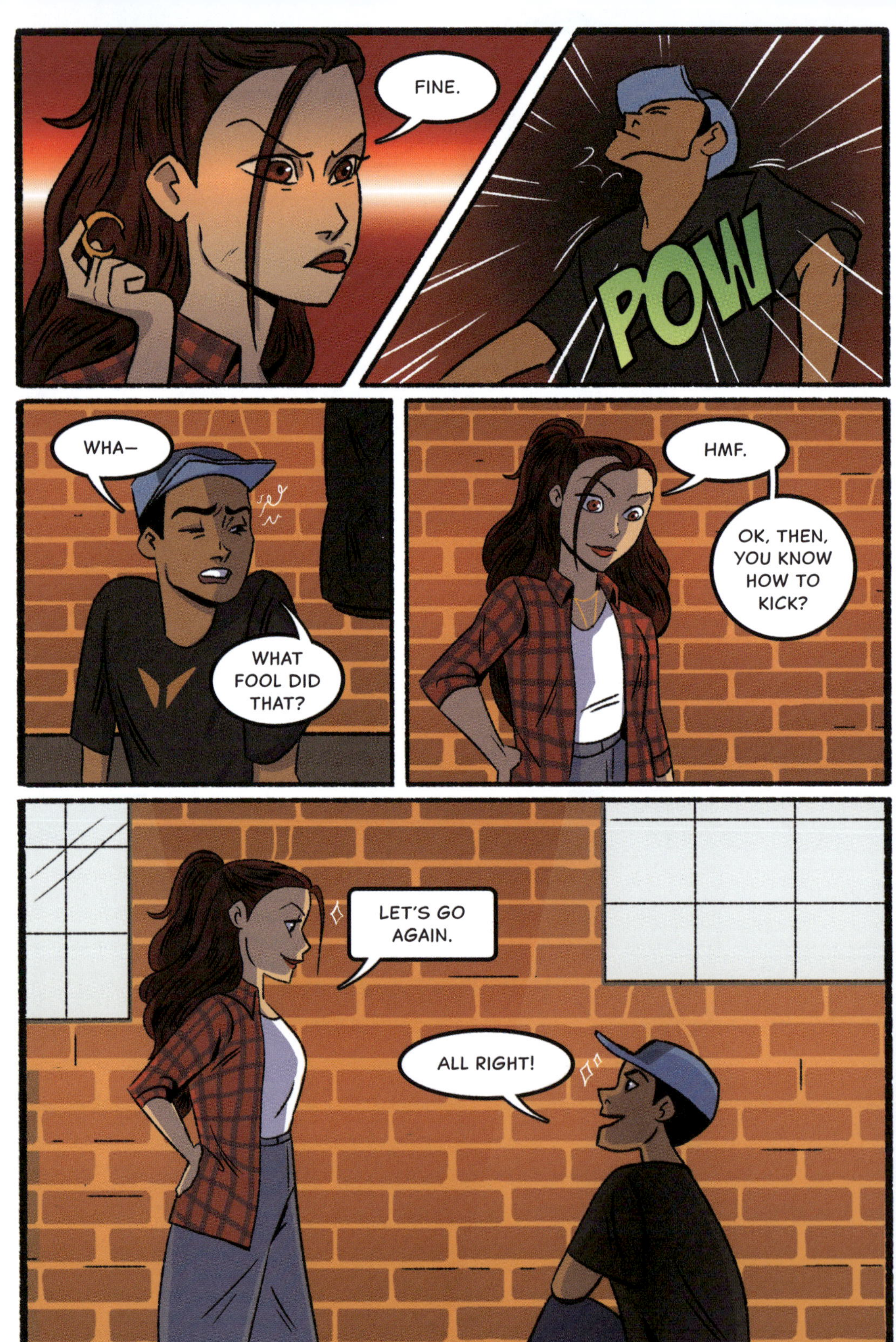
FINE.
POW
WHA—
WHAT FOOL DID THAT?
HMF.
OK, THEN, YOU KNOW HOW TO KICK?
LET'S GO AGAIN.
ALL RIGHT!

Chapter 5

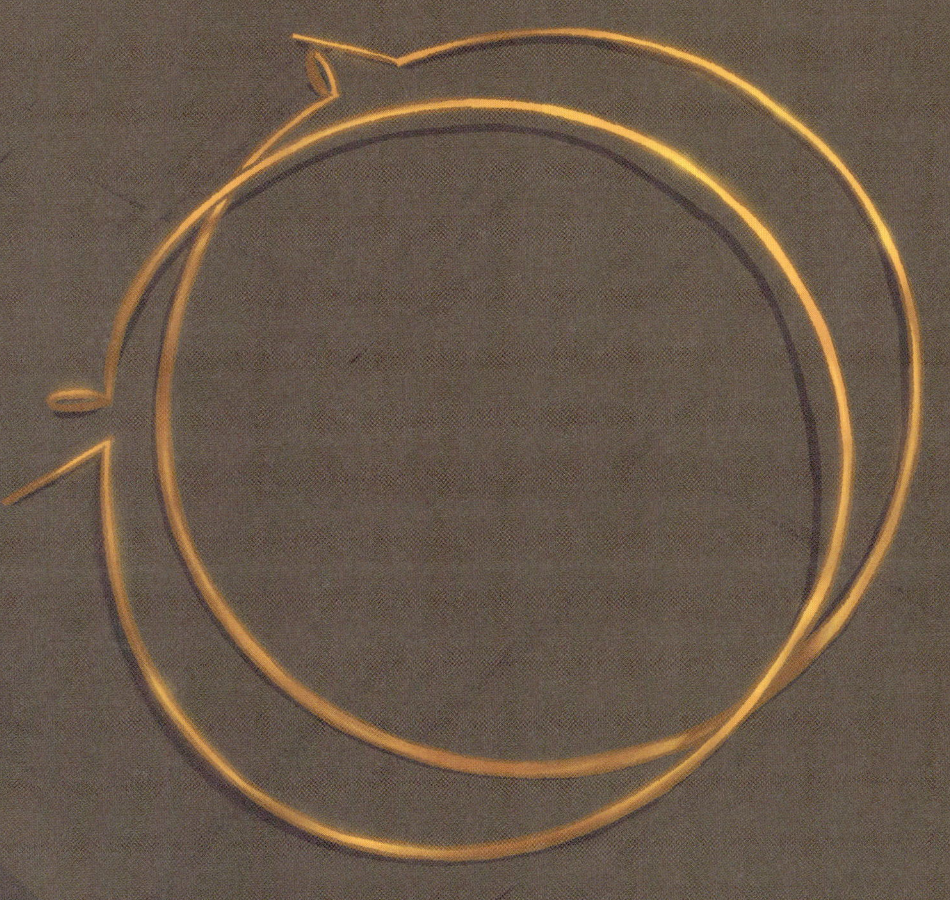

YOU SURE YOU'RE ALL RIGHT?

HAHA! SOMEONE NEEDS PROTECTION.
AND IT'S DEFINITELY NOT YOU!

HEH. THANKS AGAIN!

505
YOU'RE BACK!
HEY.

AHH. SEE YOU AT THE DIAMOND!

HEY, CHICLE. LATER.

VATO AND I ARE HEADING TO THE PARK.
YEAH?
I'LL COME WITH.

AWW, HI DOGGY!

YOU LIKE KIDS, RIGHT?
YOU SHOULD TALK TO THEM.

...SO THEN WHAT HAPPENED?
THE LITTLE GIRLS NEVER MADE IT TO THE CARNIVAL! THE EVIL WITCH, VYKA, TRICKED 'EM!
OH NO...
YEP.

THEY HAD TO CLEAN HER HOUSE FOR THE REST OF THEIR LIVES AND NEVER SAW THEIR MOMS OR DADS EVER AGAIN!
THAT'S HOW MY MOM USED TO TELL IT, AT LEAST.
ANYWAY, THAT'S WHY YOU GOTTA WATCH OUT. VYKA ALWAYS LOOKS FOR LITTLE KIDS! YOU EVER SEE ANYONE MEAN OR WEIRD, YOU REMEMBER THAT.

LIKE HIM?
WHO?

THAT GUY OVER THERE.
HE'S BEEN HERE BEFORE.

YEAH.
STAY WITH PACHUCA, VATO.

TELL US WHAT YOU KNOW.
N-NOTHING!
THEY TOLD ME TO COME HERE.
WHO?!
I DON'T KNOW, THE GUY ON THE PHONE, THEY DIDN'T TELL ME!
PULL IT OUT SLOWLY.
CALL IT.
THE NUMBER YOU HAVE CALLED IS NO LONGER IN SERVICE...

DAMMIT!
GET LOST! DON'T DO THIS AGAIN!
WHY DID YOU LET HIM GO? YOU HAD HIM!
THAT WAS *JUST* A GOON.
WE NEED THE POWER PLAYERS, NOT THE ONES ON THE BOTTOM.
YOU CAME DOWN HERE, LIKE US?
I WANT TO HELP.
WE'RE HAVING A MEETING TOMORROW, IF YOU'RE SERIOUS.

ISABEL'S BROTHER WAS TAKEN RIGHT OUT OF THEIR FRONT YARD AFTER WE CAME DOWN TO SAN DIEGO.
YOU BETTER BE SERIOUS, BECAUSE WE'RE THE ONLY PEOPLE WHO ARE.

HOPE WE SEE YOU TOMORROW, EAST LOS.

...ANOTHER CHILD HAS BEEN REPORTED MISSING FROM THE BOYLE HEIGHTS COMMUNITY.

I CAME HERE TO HELP, AND I'M NOT DOING ANYTHING.

OF COURSE YOU ARE.
YOU'RE SEARCHING, RIGHT?

YOU'RE TRYING.
THAT'S MORE THAN MOST PEOPLE CAN SAY.

AH.

WELL, AT LEAST I'M DOING MORE THAN THIS LOAF.
VATO, YOU'RE THE LAZIEST BOY I'VE EVER MET.
...VATO'S A GIRL. YOU KNOW THAT, RIGHT?

WAIT, WHAT?!
HUH.

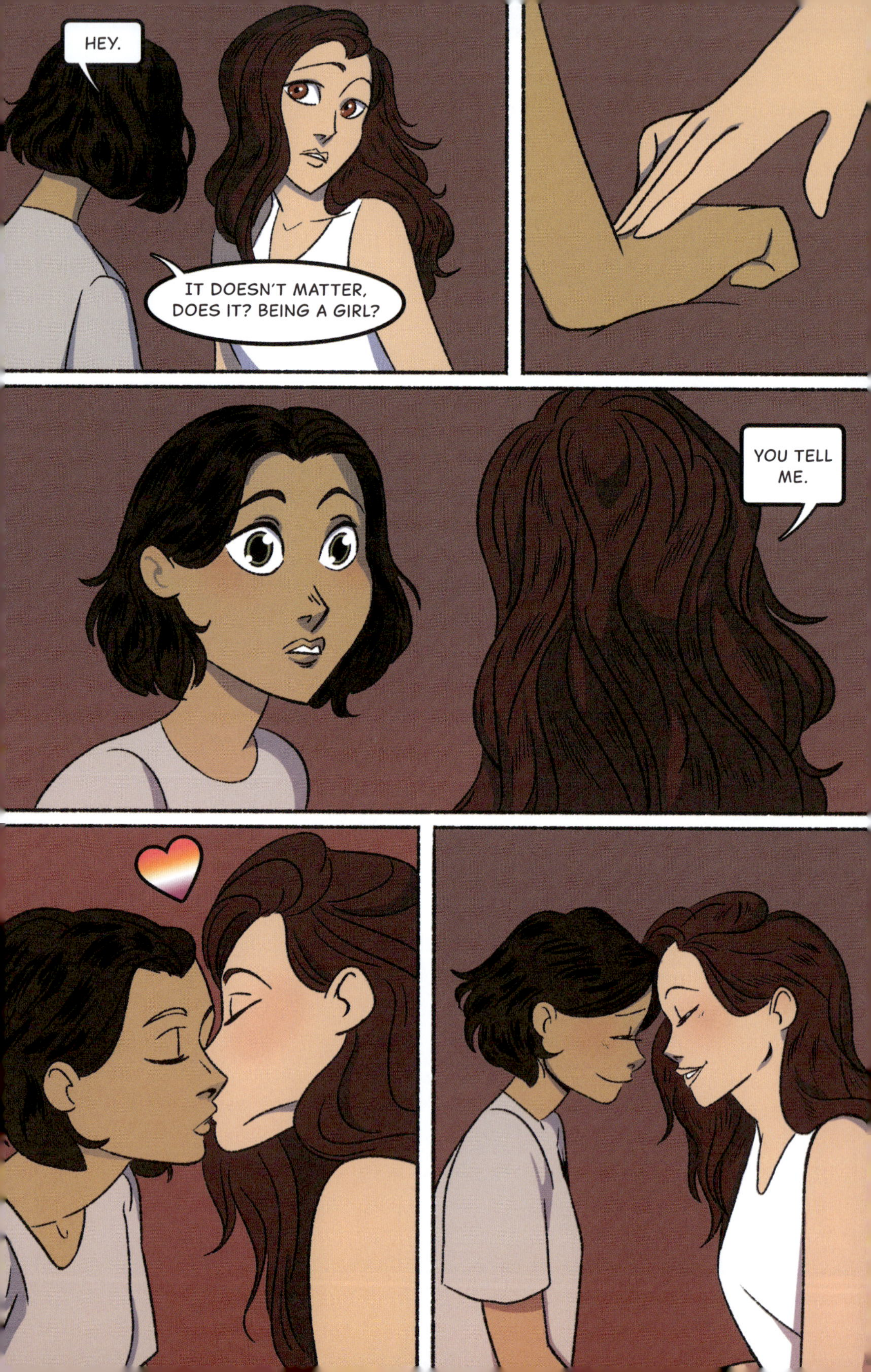

HEY.
IT DOESN'T MATTER, DOES IT? BEING A GIRL?

Chapter 6

YOUR DONATION WAS LATE THIS MONTH, ARCHBISHOP.
...YES, OF COURSE. THE YOUTH CHOIR WILL BE READY FOR THE GALA.
DON'T BE LATE AGAIN.

PACHUCA'S CLASS IS ALMOST OVER, PERRITA.

I'M STILL GONNA CALL YOU VATO, BY THE WAY.
SCREECH!

HOLA, CHOLA!
GREAT, THIS GUY AGAIN.

HEARD YOU GOT A NEW RIDE.

I USED TO REV HER ENGINE.

GET LOST, LOSER.
SHE'LL GET BORED SOON ENOUGH.

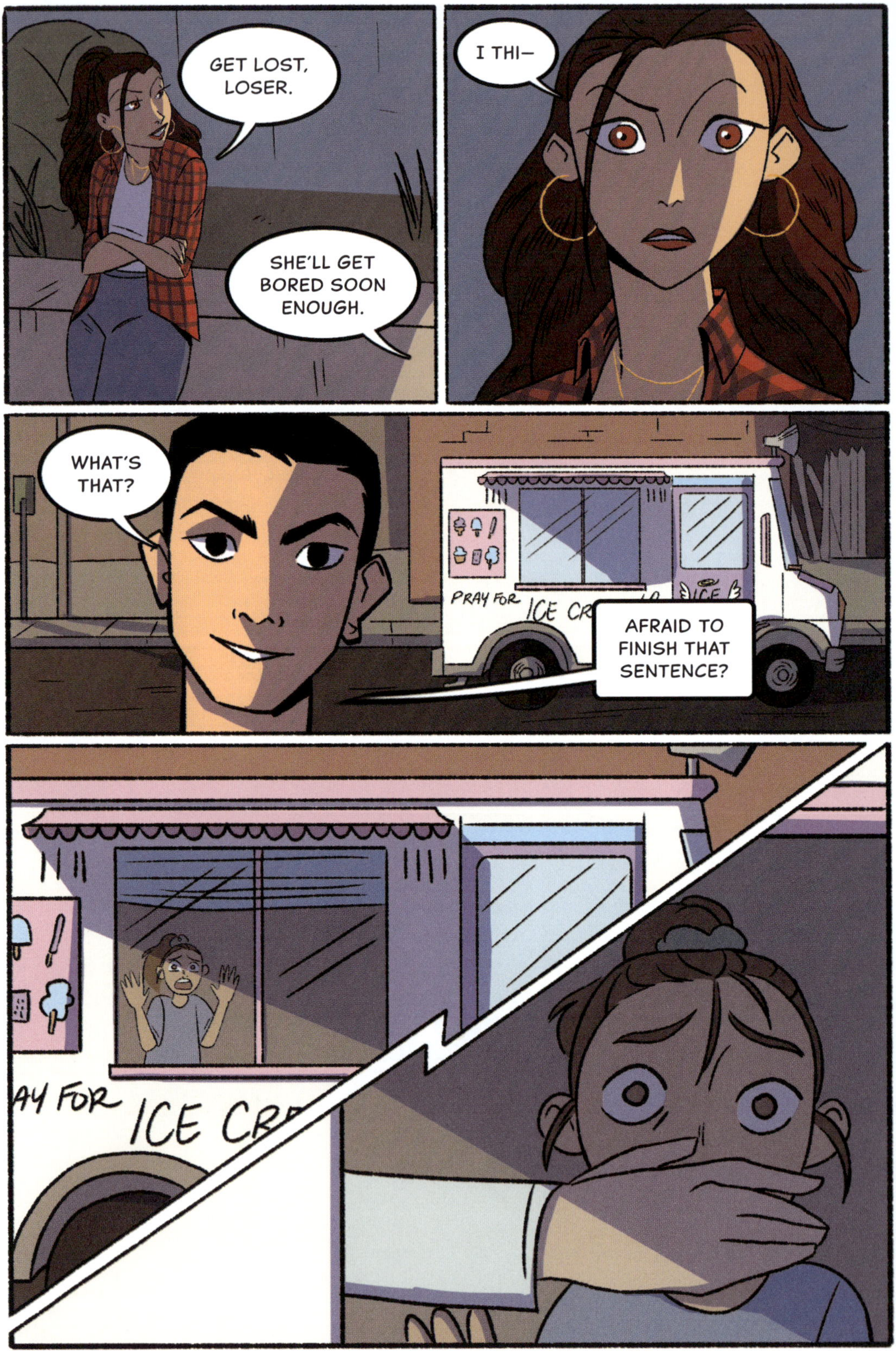

I THI—

WHAT'S THAT?
PRAY FOR ICE CR
AFRAID TO FINISH THAT SENTENCE?

THERE'S
A KID IN
THERE!

WHAT?

HEY, DON'T
WALK AWAY
WHEN—
SHUT UP, I
DON'T HAVE TIME
FOR THIS!

IS THERE
A PROBLEM?

...NO, OFFICER.
ACTUALLY, YES.
THAT ICE CREAM
TRUCK BEHIND
YOU!

IS THAT A PIT BULL?
GRR...
THEY'RE GETTING AWAY!
SHE'S HARMLESS.
MA'AM, YOU NEED TO LEASH THAT DO—
WOOF! WOOF!

BANG!
BANG!

SH-SHE WAS HARMLESS; THEY'RE GETTING AWAY...
I NEED TO BORROW THIS!
HEY!

STOP!
SERIOUSLY?
VRRRMMMM
MC8
SCREECH!
CRASH!

GET US OUT OF HERE!
IS THE KID OK?
UHH...
SHE'S GONE!
LET'S GET YOU HOME.

HERE.
THANKS.

I DID EVERYTHING I COULD, BUT...
I KNOW.

I COULDN'T SAVE VATO. I'M SO SORRY.

I'M SORRY.
WHAT YOU'RE GOING THROUGH RIGHT NOW WILL SET YOUR CARDS FOR THE FUTURE...
YOU'RE STRONG, BUT OUT THERE...
YOUR CHOICES WILL CREATE HARDSHIPS. BUT KNOW IT WILL WORK OUT.

YOU HAVE TO BE BETTER THAN ME.

SIT TIGHT UNTIL YOUR TRIAL.

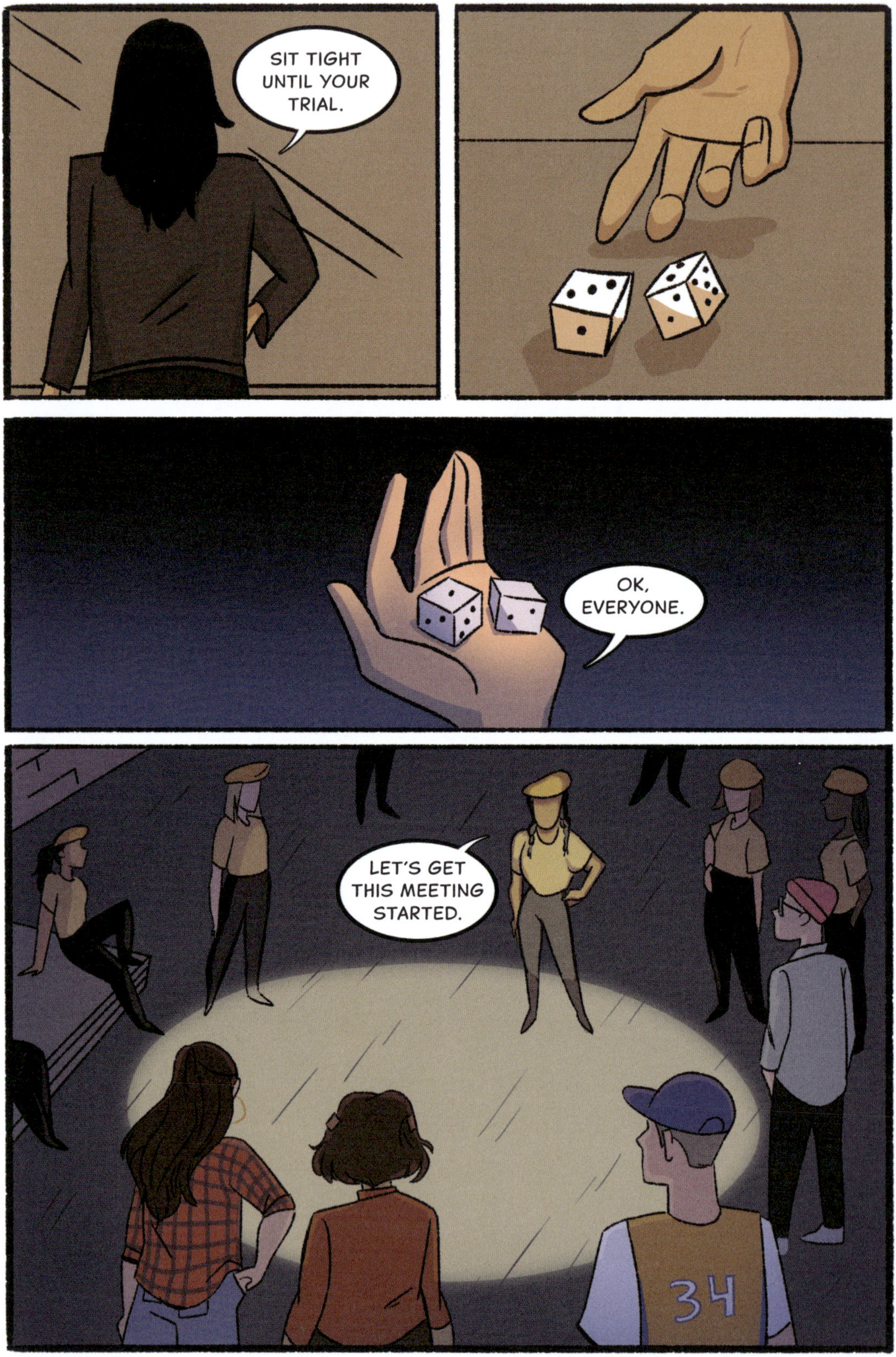

OK, EVERYONE.

LET'S GET THIS MEETING STARTED.

LA MONJA IS HOSTING AN EVENT. WE'RE NEVER GONNA GET A BETTER CHANCE TO GET THE KIDS BACK.

BUT WE CAN'T JUST CHARGE IN AND TAKE THEM.
WHAT ELSE ARE WE GONNA DO, *BUY* THEM BACK?
THAT'S JUST FUNDING THE CYCLE.

THEY STEAL KIDS, WE STEAL THEM RIGHT BACK.
WHAT'S THIS EVENT?
IT'S AT LA MONJA'S SANCTUARY IN THE WOODS.

IT'S HIDDEN IN THE HILLS. ON PAPER, IT'S HOSTING A CHARITY GALA.
THESE GUESTS ARE THE 1 PERCENTERS.
THEY ARRIVE AT SUNDOWN AT 7, AND THEIR SEATS ARE ASSIGNED WITH CODE WORDS.
HOW DO YOU KNOW ALL THIS?

HEY, RUCA!

CHICLE!
THEY HAVE NO IDEA THE DOPE WHO CLEANS THE PLACE HAS BEEN GETTING INTEL THE WHOLE TIME.
LUCKY, RIGHT?

WE NEED TO FIGURE OUT HOW TO GET IN.

I MAY HAVE AN IDEA.

IT'S A LITTLE DANGEROUS...

I DON'T WANT YOU TO GO.
I'M GOING.
HOW YOU GONNA FIGHT?
YOU HAVE TO STAY OUT OF TROUBLE. YOU HAVE SCHOOL! IF THINGS GO BAD...

YOU HAVE A *FUTURE!*

YOU HAVE A FUTURE TOO.
THE PAST DOESN'T NEED TO INFLUENCE YOUR PLAY NOW, RIGHT?

ROLL THE DICE.
PACHUCA...

AFTER ALL THIS, I'M... I GOTTA GET GOING.
AND YOU GOTTA GRADUATE.

I KNOW.
I'M STILL GOING TOMORROW.

Chapter 7

HOLY WATER
HOLY WATER
GLUG!
LET'S MOSEY.

HEY, CARNAL!

IF YOU CAN ALL FIND YOUR SEATS...
WELCOME ESTEEMED GUESTS.
WE ARE SO HAPPY TO HAVE YOU AT OUR LADY OF SACRIFICIAL HEARTS CHURCH.
THIS EVENING, WE WILL HAVE A VERY SPECIAL PERFORMANCE...

DOES THIS HOLY WATER SMELL WEIRD TO YOU?
HUMBALDO

SNIFF

THUMP
GUESS SO.
COAST IS CLEAR!
HOLY WATER

AS WE PRACTICED, CHILDREN...
YAWN
$$$$
$$$$
$$$
CLINK

FOOM!
COUGH
COUGH
ZZZ
ZZZ
PARTY'S OVER.

THIS IS A PRIVATE EVENT!
SHOOT, REALLY?
SEEMS LIKE YOUR GUARD'S A LITTLE TIED UP.
RUN ALONG, CHILDREN.
YOU CAN CALL THE COPS, IF YOU WANT.
THIS IS GREAT EVIDENCE, BY THE WAY.
ARCHBISHOP, IF YOU'D KINDLY RETIRE. I HAVE SOME CLEANING TO ATTEND TO.

HE CAN'T GET AWAY!
WE HAVE TO STOP IT FROM THE TOP!
THE KIDS!
HELLO?
I'M HERE TO HELP!
AND WHAT HELP COULD THE LIKES OF YOU PROVIDE?
I'M GOING TO MAKE SURE YOU GO TO PRISON!
WITH WHAT POWER? THE LAW? WHY, YOU FIT THE PROFILE OF A CRIMINAL FAR MORE THAN I DO.

DO YOUR PARENTS KNOW YOU'RE PART OF A GANG?
SUCH A PITY.
SHHH~
DID YOU JUST...
SHUSH ME?
YOU HAVE THE GIFT?
GIFT? WHAT GIFT?
ATTACK HER!

STOP!
WAKE UP!
SMACK!
THUMP
WHAT GIFT?
DID YOUR MOM GIVE YOU SOMETHING TOO?
NO, I *TOOK* MY GIFT FROM HER!
I RETAIN THE POWER OF FREE WILL.
I ALWAYS WIN, NO MATTER THE COST!

TAKE IT DOWN FROM THE TOP...
WHERE?
THERE!
STOP!
HEY!
POW!
PHEW.
CAN I GET SOME ZIP TIES OVER HERE?

I DON'T HAVE THE LAW BEHIND ME...
THAT'S TOO BAD. BECAUSE WINNING IS MY SPECIALTY.
BUT I DO HAVE JUSTICE.
CRRRRRACK
CRASH

...DANG, WHAT'D I MISS?
KARMA.
ISABEL CALLED THE CAVALRY IN. THEY'RE TAKING ALL THE KIDS HO—EURGH!

WHAT ABOUT THE BUYERS?
POLICE
POLICE
OH, WE MADE SURE THEY'VE GOT THEIR BIDS CLOSE TO THEIR CHESTS.
...THOUGH I DON'T THINK THIS WAS THE COLLECTION THEY WERE EXPECTING.

YOU'RE OK NOW. LET'S GO HOME.

A MIRACLE, KISMET, AND COSMIC JUSTICE ARE JUST SOME OF THE THINGS RELIEVED FAMILIES ARE CALLING WHAT HAPPENED OVER THE WEEKEND.

THANKS TO EVERYONE!! YOU DON'T KNOW WHAT ZIGGY MEANS TO ME.
S.W.A.T. ARRESTED FIFTY INDIVIDUALS INVOLVED...
FINALLY, A GOOD STORY.

BARRIO LOGAN
BUS STOP

HEY, I WANTED TO SEE YOU OFF!
THIS IS FOR YOU!

THANKS.

WHEN I GRADUATE, I CAN COME AND VISIT HER AND YOU.
VISITATION RIGHTS, HUH?

THE END.

CONCEPT ART

jaguar shaped
- smirky smile
- mouth wide
- top & bottom lip same size
rotate top of bridge & nose tip
med-closeups
SIMPLIFY FOR DISTANCE

About the Author

KAYDEN PHOENIX IS A WRITER FROM LOS ANGELES, CALIFORNIA. SHE CREATED THE FIRST LATINA SUPERHERO TEAM IN COMIC BOOK HISTORY: A LA BRAVA. "A BIG PART OF MY LIFE'S PURPOSE IS TO GIVE VOICE TO STORIES AS MULTIFACETED, ATYPICAL, AND DIVERSE AS THE PEOPLE WE FIND IN THE REAL WORLD."